The way he said her name was like a soft caress...

"Deanna."

Every nerve in her body was suddenly awakened. Her heart quickened. Ever since they'd danced together, her imagination had worked overtime on all the seductive things he might say to her in a raw sweep of desire.

He said softly, "I want you to know that you are the most remarkable woman I've ever met."

Remarkable? *Remarkable?* Deanna turned the word over in her mind as a kind of hysterical laughter caught in her throat. Not devastating. Not appealing. Not sexy. Not charming. Just remarkable. This definitely wasn't the kind of compliment she'd hoped for from a man who had turned her romantic fantasies upside down.

She managed a brittle smile. "And I think you're very upstanding, Dr. Sherman."

"Upstanding?" he echoed.

Two could play at this game. "And I admire you because you're ethical, and principled, and honorable, and—"

She never finished, because in one swift movement he pulled her to him and his mouth came down on hers and took her breath with a long, questing kiss.

Dear Harlequin Intrigue Reader,

Sunscreen, a poolside lounge—and Harlequin Intrigue: the perfect recipe for great summer escapes!

This month's sizzling selection begins with *The Stranger Next Door* (#573) by Joanna Wayne, the second in her RANDOLPH FAMILY TIES miniseries. Langley Randolph is the kind of Texan who can't resist a woman in trouble. Can he help unlock a beautiful stranger's memories...before a killer catches up with her first?

Little Penny Drake is an *Innocent Witness* (#574) to a murder in this suspenseful yet tender story by Leona Karr. The child's desperate mother, Deanna, seeks the help of Dr. Steve Sherman. Can Steve unlock her daughter's secrets...and Deanna's heart?

Dr. Jonas Shades needs a woman to play his wife. Cathlynn O'Connell is the perfect candidate, but with time running out, he has no choice but to blackmail his bride. Each minute in Jonas's presence brings Cathlynn closer to understanding her enigmatic "husband" *and* closer to danger! Don't miss *Blackmailed Bride* (#575) by Sylvie Kurtz.

Bestselling Harlequin American Romance author Tina Leonard joins Harlequin Intrigue with a story of spine-tingling suspense and dramatic romance. She's created the small town of Crookseye Canyon, Texas, as the backdrop for *A Man of Honor* (#576). Cord Greer must marry his brother's woman to keep her and her unborn baby safe. But is it fear that drives Tessa Draper into Cord's arms, or is it something more than Cord had hoped for?

Indulge yourself and find out this summer—and all year long!

Sincerely,

Denise O'Sullivan
Associate Senior Editor
Harlequin Intrigue

Innocent Witness
Leona Karr

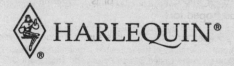

TORONTO • NEW YORK • LONDON
AMSTERDAM • PARIS • SYDNEY • HAMBURG
STOCKHOLM • ATHENS • TOKYO • MILAN • MADRID
PRAGUE • WARSAW • BUDAPEST • AUCKLAND

ISBN 0-373-22574-1

INNOCENT WITNESS

Copyright © 2000 by Leona Karr

This edition published by arrangement with Harlequin Books S.A.

® and TM are trademarks of the publisher. Trademarks indicated with
® are registered in the United States Patent and Trademark Office, the
Canadian Trade Marks Office and in other countries.

Visit us at www.eHarlequin.com

Printed in U.S.A.

ABOUT THE AUTHOR

Leona Karr loves to read and write, and her favorite books are romantic suspense. Every book she writes is an exciting discovery as she finds the right combination of romance and intrigue. She has authored over thirty novels, many of which, like *Innocent Witness*, are set in her home state, Colorado. When she's not reading and writing, she thoroughly enjoys spoiling her eight beautiful granddaughters.

Books by Leona Karr

HARLEQUIN INTRIGUE

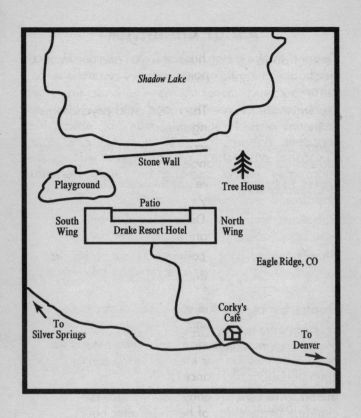

Shadow Lake

Stone Wall

Tree House

Playground

Patio

South
Wing

Drake Resort Hotel

North
Wing

Eagle Ridge, CO

Corky's
Cafe

To
Silver Springs

To
Denver

CAST OF CHARACTERS

Deanna Drake —Her husband was murdered and her daughter hasn't spoken since. She needs a miracle.

Dr. Steve Sherman —The noted child psychologist is known for performing miracles.

Penny Drake —The secrets locked in the four-year-old's mind may be dangerous to all.

Travis Sherman —Steve's seven-year-old son appoints himself Penny's protector.

Bob Anderson —He's Deanna's right-hand man— how badly does he want to be more?

Sheriff Janson —He's convinced Deanna knows more than she's saying, and he won't take what she does say seriously.

Dillon —What does the crusty bartender know about Deanna's husband's clandestine activities?

Maude Beaker —The gruff cook won't stand for anyone messing in her kitchen. Is she trying to keep people at a distance?

Susan Whitcomb —Penny's nanny makes clandestine meetings of her own after hours.

Jeffery —The hotel desk clerk jealously guards his relationship with Susan.

Roger —The ex-ski bum is another suitor for Susan's hand.

Hobo —The dog seems to understand Penny's unspoken communications.

With love to Dorothy McClane,
a special friend, good neighbor
and loyal fan.

Chapter One

Night shadows rippled in the waters of the lake and flickered through the needled branches of tall ponderosa pine trees standing at the back of the mountain hotel. A small girl, wandering sleepily onto her second-floor balcony, heard murmuring voices and saw two men walking toward a stone wall at the edge of the water. As the child recognized her father, she leaned against the railing and called out to him, but her voice was lost in the muffled sound of gunshot. Her father slumped to the ground, and in paralyzed terror, the little girl watched as the man dragged Papa by the legs into the darkness of encroaching trees.

Dr. Steve Sherman touched the button on his intercom and alerted his secretary that he was ready for his next patient. As an attractive fair-haired woman and a little girl about four years old opened the door and came in, he walked toward them and offered his hand.

"Steve Sherman. I'm glad to meet you, Mrs. Drake."

"My pleasure, Doctor," she responded politely. She had arresting blue eyes that regarded him rather coolly under thick, crescent-shaped eyelashes.

"And this pretty little girl must be Penny?" Steve

smiled down at the blond, curly-headed child who was staring at him with unblinking eyes. Her posture was stiff, guarded, and the little girl's tiny fingers visibly tightened on her mother's hand.

The child had been referred to him by the Colorado Children's Mental Health Clinic, and the unusual circumstances that had triggered her emotional withdrawal intrigued him. As a well-known child psychologist specializing in children's trauma, Steve had gained a reputation as an authority on using play therapy as a means of defining and releasing emotional conflicts in children.

He'd carefully read the thick case-study file on the little girl, verifying that since the death of her father four months earlier, Penny Drake's behavior had become erratic, defensive and antisocial, a complete reversal from the happy, outgoing child she had been before the tragedy. Without any promise of taking the case, he'd agreed to an initial interview with the child and her mother.

Ignoring the way Penny turned her head away and refused to make eye contact with him, Steve said warmly, "I've been looking forward to meeting you, Penny."

No response.

"Thank you, Doctor, for seeing us on such short notice." Deanna answered politely, while at the same time trying to control her disappointment. Dr. Steve Sherman was not at all what Deanna had expected or hoped for. The casually dressed doctor looked more like he belonged on a golf course than in the office treating children who desperately needed help. He wore a polo shirt, open at the neck, allowing glimpses of chest hair that matched the slightly curling reddish-brown shocks of hair falling over his forehead. Tan slacks and loafers added to the youthful look, and Deanna guessed him to be in his early thirties. Her heart sank. She had expected a much older man. She desperately needed someone who was professionally competent and serious about helping her little girl.

"I assume that the Children's Clinic sent you Penny's records?" Deanna continued, endeavoring to put some kind of formality into the interview. Handling matters in an efficient, organized way was her nature and had been partly responsible for her success as a businesswoman.

"Why don't we sit down?" Steve suggested pleasantly without answering, mentally noting her let's-get-down-to-business tone. The elegance of her short layered blond hair and the way she held her head gave her a regal quality that matched her beautifully shaped mouth and firm chin. Deanna Drake's negative vibes were a warning to ready himself for a challenge. *This might be interesting.*

"Have a seat...or a pillow, rather," he invited as he pointed to a low round table surrounded by soft cushions placed in the center of the large room.

Deanna tried to keep her expression from revealing her reaction. Was the initial interview with this psychologist going to take place here, in this room which held no resemblance to a regular office? Except for a well-worn floral couch and a window seat, the only places to sit were the floor cushions and a few children's chairs scattered around the room. A desk, a chair and some file cabinets were pushed into one corner, and the rest of the space was taken up with all kinds of children's paraphernalia. Everything was shoved onto shelves without any visible sign of organization. A line of framed diplomas on the wall shared crowded space with large baseball posters, Mother Goose pictures, Sesame Street characters and childish artwork. How could the psychologist possibly expect to conduct a professional interview sitting on floor cushions around a table that held a pitcher of chocolate milk, a plate of cookies and several stuffed animals and puppets?

"The pillows are more comfortable than they look," Steve reassured her, noting her hesitation. "Of course, Mrs. Drake, we can go into the conference room and conduct the interview there if you'd be more at ease...?" He let the sentence dangle like an unspoken challenge.

Deanna met his eyes without a flicker of her long lashes. "This will be fine." She certainly wasn't going to let this unorthodox therapist make her lose her composure.

"Good," he said approvingly as if she'd passed some sort of test.

As Deanna sat down on one of the floor pillows, she was thankful that she had decided to wear white slacks and a yellow shirtwaist blouse instead of a summer dress. Trying to keep her legs covered with a short skirt would have been totally embarrassing. She gave Penny's hand a reassuring squeeze as she eased her daughter down on the pillow next to her. Taking a deep breath, she tried to quell her nervousness.

Steve chose a cushion across the table from them, sat down and wound his long legs into a cross-legged sitting position. "Would you like a glass of chocolate milk?" he asked as if they were at some Mad Hatter's tea party.

Deanna silently fumed, *No, I don't want any milk. I want to know if you can help my daughter.* She hadn't driven fifty miles down a mountain road from her home in Eagle Ridge to Denver, and also canceled some important business engagements, so she could play tea party. Without comment, Deanna took the glass he offered.

From the way Penny was watching her mother, Steve knew that the little girl had already picked up, with the intuitive perception of children, that her mother didn't like Dr. Steve Sherman. He sighed. *Not a good beginning.* The first hurdle in successfully treating any child was gaining the parent's confidence, and it didn't take a degree in psychology to know that he was losing the first inning with Deanna Drake.

"I hope Penny likes chocolate milk," Steve said as he set a glass in front of her. The child's guarded look went from her mother to Steve and back to the milk. Then she set her little lips in a stubborn line and made no move to touch the glass.

Steve watched her while pretending to give all his attention to his own glass. As much as the little girl might want to drink the chocolate milk, she wouldn't touch it. *Why? What held her back? What was fueling her willpower and resistance?* Although he'd had remarkable success working with traumatized children, he knew that when a psychosis was deeply-seated, the psyche protected itself at all costs.

Steve had read newspaper accounts of Benjamin Drake's murder in the file, and he knew that they had found the child whimpering in a terrified state on her balcony, but whatever had happened on the night that Penny's father had been shot still remained a mystery. She must have been a witness to the crime. Who knew what secrets were buried in Penelope Drake's pretty little head? And equally important, would the child be put

in danger if he was successful in breaking her silence
about them?

"Would you like a cookie, Penny?" he asked, plac-
ing one beside the little girl's untouched glass of milk.
Then he took one for himself and laughed as he sniffed
it. "Don't they smell good. Freshly baked."

Deanna tried to control her impatience. When she'd
heard about Dr. Steve Sherman, the child psychologist
who had just moved to the Denver area from California,
her hopes had risen like released balloons. Maybe he
was the miracle she'd been praying for. Maybe he had
the expertise needed to help Penny be herself again. But
as Deanna studied the man across the table from her,
her high hopes were more like helium balloons sagging
from slow leaks. The relaxed psychologist's attention
was on pouring chocolate milk and offering cookies, as
if the gravity of the situation completely escaped him.

Steve met her frown with a smile. He knew exactly
what she was thinking. Deanna Drake had come to him
because she was desperate, and he could tell that she
had already written him off as another false and painful
disappointment. No doctor in a white coat. No clipboard
filled with charts. No reassuring medical trappings. A
waste of time. Disappointment radiated from her.

"You live in Eagle Ridge, Colorado?" he asked in
a conversational tone, as if they had all the time in the
world.

"Yes." *It's in the file,* Deanna silently replied as her
chest tightened. Everything was in the records, includ-
ing her hotel management degree and her five-year marriage to a man fifteen years her senior.

"I'm not sure where Eagle Ridge is." He raised a
questioning dark brown eyebrow. "I guess you know

I'm new to Colorado. I'm determined to take some time and enjoy these magnificent mountains.''

"Eagle Ridge is northwest of Denver, about fifty miles. It's a small mountain town that survives on tourist dollars winter and summer. I inherited a small resort hotel from my late husband. Of course, if you've read Penny's case history, you know all of that.''

"Sounds like a wonderful place to raise children,'' he said, ignoring the slight edge to her voice.

"I can't imagine living anywhere else,'' she admitted, and then added quickly, "But I'd move in a minute if I thought it would help Penny.''

"Those are my sentiments as a parent exactly,'' he agreed. "That's why I left California. I wanted something better for my son, Travis. I'm also a single parent. I lost my wife when Travis was less than two years old. His grandmother helped raise him, but she passed away last year, so it's just the two of us.''

So the handsome Dr. Sherman was a widower, thought Deanna. Why they were spending time on his personal life, she didn't know, but the fact that he also had a child was, in a way, reassuring. "How old is your son?''

"Travis is seven. I'm hoping he'll really take to Colorado. I've promised to take him hiking and fishing this summer, and next winter we'll hit the ski slopes.'' He grinned at Penny. "He's never thrown a snowball. And he wants me to buy him a sled. He's always singing that song about Frosty—you know the one I mean, Penny?''

The little girl's eyes flickered slightly with interest, but she didn't answer. Deanna silently fumed. Where was he going with all of this chitchat? Since her father's murder, Penny seldom interacted with anyone or anything.

"Do you want me to sing it for you?" he asked with a grin. The change in the little girl's stare was almost imperceptible, but Steve's trained eyes caught it. *So far, so good. Penny Drake is bright and receptive.* He leaned toward her and whispered in a confidential tone, "I don't know all the words. Do you?"

Her mouth remained closed.

Deanna watched them both. Steve didn't seem to notice Penny's silence or feel rebuffed by it. He carefully broke his cookie into tiny bite-size chunks before eating each piece with delighted exaggeration. "Mmm, good." He winked at her, but Penny's expression remained guarded, and she continued to sit rigidly without touching cookie or milk.

Deanna deliberately looked at her watch, a pointed reminder that Dr. Sherman was using up time for which she was paying. She was impatient with the psychologist's apparent lack of direction and his total disregard for the gravity of the situation. Disappointment created a sick feeling in the pit of her stomach.

At that moment, there were three short knocks at an inner door and Steve smiled as if he'd been expecting someone. He called out, "Come in, Travis."

As a small boy poked his head into the room, Steve motioned him over to the table. "Come on in, Travis. I want you to meet Penny and her mother, Mrs. Drake."

Travis had the same wide grin as his father, and the same wayward russet hair that had a will of its own. His face was lightly freckled, and dark eyelashes and eyebrows framed an alert pair of brown eyes.

"Hi," the boy said brightly.

"Would you like some cookies and milk, Travis?"

"Sure," he said as he plopped down on a pillow next to Penny. Then he eagerly reached into the pile of stuffed animals in the center of the table, and drew out two puppets, Kermit the Frog and Cookie Monster. "Here", he said, thrusting the blue puppet into Penny's hands. "You can feed Cookie Monster. See, he's got a pocket for cookies. Take one for him, and one for you." Leaning toward her, he said in a conspirator's whisper, "That way you get to eat two."

Penny took the puppet, and her expression changed to one of wonder as she watched Travis put a cookie in Kermit the Frog's lap and pop one in his own mouth. "Peanut butter cookies are the best!" he announced happily.

"Don't talk with your mouth full," Steve chided gently, silently patting himself on the back. *Good move, Steve, old boy. Using Travis to help diagnose the little girl's social patterns looks like a winner.* Penny still didn't eat a cookie or feed the puppet, but her listless manner had been replaced by a notable flicker of interest as she watched Travis.

"Son, remember the pictures of those huge Colorado mountains?" Steve asked casually. "That's where Penny lives."

Travis's brown eyes widened. "Really? Wow!"

"I bet Penny would like to see those clay mountains you made for our train set."

"Sure." He put down his puppet and took the one back he'd given Penny. He grabbed one of her hands and urged her to her feet. "You can be the engineer, Penny. I'll show you how."

Deanna stiffened. In the last four months, Penny had never willingly had anything to do with other children. Numerous attempts to get her to socialize with girls and boys her age had failed. She always hung back, guarded and silent, taking in everything with those candid eyes of hers, but never participating. Deanna couldn't believe it when Penny didn't even look in her direction for reassurance, but followed the boy over to a large train set on a sawhorse table.

Unable to hide her surprise, Deanna murmured, "I don't believe it."

"Believe what?" Steve casually took a sip of chocolate milk, but Deanna detected a gleam of satisfaction as his gaze locked with hers over the rim of his glass.

She didn't know how he had subtly managed to create a safe atmosphere for Penny, but she did know it was time to let go of the reins. "All right, Dr. Sherman. Tell me about play therapy."

"The technique is really very simple," he said, wiping off a chocolate-milk mustache. "Children are encouraged to use toys and other materials to reveal what is being repressed or controlled. Once they reveal those inner workings, we can answer the fears that have been responsible for changes in personality and behavior."

"But Penny has a roomful of toys," Deanna protested. "She has people willing to play all kinds of games with her."

"And they allow Penny her own space—just to be?"

"We don't push her to do anything."

"Isn't it true that for four months you've been pushing her to be the little girl she once was?" he asked frankly.

Deanna's spine stiffened. How dare he question her loving concern for her daughter? "It's true that I've been searching for a way to heal my child's emotional wounds and return her to normalcy."

"Pushing too hard?" he suggested quietly. "I know

how hard it is for parents to relax and be patient when there's so much at stake. I'm afraid there aren't any quick fixes for deep emotional traumas. It takes time, patience and love.''

Deanna looked at the two children, their heads together, one yellow as corn silk, the other the russet brown of autumn leaves. Her eyes suddenly misted, and she lowered them quickly, blinking rapidly to hold back the tears. She was startled when he reached across the table and laid his hand on hers.

He didn't say anything, and for a brief moment she drew in the warmth of the unexpected touch. Then she took her hand away. Life had not been easy, and she knew that she could be stiff-necked about a lot of things, but she prided herself on being willing to concede when she'd been mistaken. She didn't need to understand why and how this man dealt so successfully with children. She took a deep breath to steady her voice as she asked, "Will you work with my daughter, Dr. Sherman?"

"There are no guarantees."

"I know, but you can try. You don't impress me as someone who runs away from challenges."

He chuckled. "Are you trying to turn my own psychology back on me, Mrs. Drake?"

"Deanna," she corrected with a smile. "Yes, I am. What do you say? Just tell me what's involved—the number of weekly sessions—and I'll have Penny here. I can arrange to stay in town two or three days in a row. Luckily, I have a good hotel manager who can handle things in my absence. Can we start right away?"

"Whoa." He smiled as he held up his hand in a stopping fashion. "I'll need time just getting acquainted before we have serious sessions. Slower is often better when working with children.''

"I understand." Nodding, she forced herself to curb her impatience. "You set the pace and we'll hold to it."

"Unfortunately, I'm clearing my schedule for the month of June. I won't be back in the office until the first of July."

Her heart took a familiar plunge. Another frustrating delay. Another heartbreaking marking of time.

"I am sorry," he apologized. "You see, I've promised Travis a summer vacation in the mountains. I couldn't break my word."

"Where are you going?" Deanna asked evenly as her mind instantly started racing like a runaway truck on one of Colorado's mountain passes.

"We haven't quite decided."

"May I make a suggestion? You and Travis could be guests at my resort hotel for part of your vacation." She smiled at him. "Eagle Ridge has beautiful scenery, a river for rafting, a lake for fishing and dozens of other mountain activities. You could stay at the hotel for as much of your vacation as you like. In exchange for my hospitality, you could spend some time with Penny. What better place for your getting-acquainted sessions?"

Her smooth, take-charge manner amused Steve, and he liked the way her eyes sparkled and her cheeks flushed pink with excitement. Deanna Drake had been attractive before, but now her face glowed.

He had to admit, her suggestion certainly had its merits, but there was only one thing wrong with it—he couldn't treat children in a vacuum. The play therapy room and everything in it was carefully selected and engineered to allow the child free expression of inner feelings. Without the proper setting, Penny wouldn't release her habitual responses, but would keep on repeating the old ones instead of forming new ones.

He tried to explain this to Deanna. "In order to make meaningful use of toys, or play therapy, the therapist must control all the variables that can possibly be controlled. Any extraneous factors can confuse what the child is revealing, or be so distracting that nothing is accomplished in the sessions. It's important to have a consistent environment and one that provides everything for the child and therapist to interact."

Deanna looked around the room, "I don't see anything in here that isn't replaceable. If you make me a list, I'll have a playroom ready that will meet your needs."

"The expense—" he began.

"Won't be close to what I'm willing to spend on Penny," she countered swiftly. "I can easily provide a nice private room in the hotel for your exclusive use. As often as it's convenient for you to have a session with Penny, the room will be ready and furnished as well as this one. That way, we could begin Penny's sessions while you and Travis enjoy an extended vacation in the mountains."

The decision was not an easy one to make. He could have insisted that the idea wasn't workable. A warning was there that he might become too emotionally involved.

There were other considerations, too. The killer of Deanna Drake's husband was still at large. As far as he knew, the case was still open, and from what he could learn, there were no real suspects and no definite motive. Since Penny's trauma was tied to the night her father was killed, Steve knew that the child's withdrawal was a way of protecting herself. If he successfully helped Penny retrieve a memory that would be a threat to whoever shot her father, what would be the consequences?

What would be the consequences if he didn't?

Later he wondered exactly what it was that made him put aside his reservations and agree. He seemed to have no choice as he looked into Deanna's hopeful face, but to smile and say, "All right. It's a deal."

Chapter Two

Deanna couldn't have been more anxious if the governor had been expected the day that Steve Sherman and Travis were due to check into the Drake Resort Hotel. Her heartbeat quickened with anticipation as she took the back stairs up to the third floor. Ever since final arrangements had been made for him and his son to spend the month of June at the hotel, her time had been filled with preparations for their visit.

Deanna had chosen a large airy room to be used as the play therapy room. Everything on the list that Dr. Sherman had given her was ready and waiting: sandbox, dollhouse, small plastic animals, cars, trucks, rubber gun and knife, easel, paints, paper, clay, play telephone, chalk, crayons, books and puzzles. In addition to the play materials, she had provided a low round table, floor cushions and a soft easy chair as faded and lumpy as the one in Dr. Sherman's therapy room. The only thing that was missing was an electric train, and he had decided that would be too tempting for Travis to leave alone.

Steve had warned Deanna not to let Penny play in the room, or even see it before her first session. ''I don't want her to have any preconceived feelings about the playroom or the toys.'' He impressed upon Deanna the need to keep the room separate from the rest of the child's normal life. ''The time spent in that room will be an experience apart from her normal activities.''

''I understand,'' she had readily agreed.

He also had warned her that what happened during play therapy was between him and her daughter.

She frowned. ''But how will I know how she's doing?''

He smiled. ''It's my job to know how she's doing, not yours. I'll share with you anything that will help me do my job. All right?''

As she gave the room one last look, she breathed a prayer that somehow, within these walls, the dark psyche that lived within her daughter would be released, and she would have her normal little daughter back again. She was just locking the playroom door when she heard footsteps on the stairs, and swung around to face Bob Henderson, her trusted hotel manager.

''Oh, Bob, it's you,'' she said, letting out her breath when she saw the thirty-year old, sandy-haired man. ''I thought…I thought maybe they'd come already.''

''Nope, not yet. Hey, girl, you're as jumpy as a cat dancing on a live wire.'' His round face creased in a frown. ''What gives? Don't you think that city doctor's going to approve of your efforts? God knows you've been knocking yourself out making sure that room is exactly like he wants it. He better not give you a bad time or I'll deal with him in short order.'' He fell in step with Deanna as she walked back down to the reception area.

Deanna laughed at his fierce expression and the way he straightened his thick shoulders as if ready to do battle. A childhood friend of hers, Bob had been her protective knight ever since high school. He had been a star football player, and still maintained a hard, muscular physique. He was already working in the hotel for her husband before the tragedy. Now he practically ran the place, and she didn't know how she'd manage without him.

"Down, boy, down," Deanna teased in a laughing fashion. "No need to show your teeth. I'm sure Dr. Sherman is going to be pleased."

"Well, he better be. Sounds to me like all the guy does is play with kid stuff and charge big bucks for it." Bob shook his head. "Are you sure he's not taking you for a ride? Giving him a free room, while dishing out good money for him to play with Penny? Sounds like a real scam to me."

"It'll be worth every cent if he can make some progress with her. Besides, I'm at my wit's end. I don't know what else to try. Nothing has worked."

Bob touched her arm. "Honey, you can't keep tearing yourself up like this. Ben wouldn't want it. You've got to get on with your life."

She knew what Bob meant by getting on with her life. He wanted to marry her. Heaven knows, he'd asked her often enough in the last four months, but the answer was always the same. She didn't want to marry Bob Henderson, or anybody else. Marriage hadn't been that terrific the first time around. The only good thing that had come out of it was Penny. Deanna wasn't about to lose her freedom again, even to someone as nice and loyal as Bob Henderson.

Bob disappeared into the office while Deanna lingered a moment in the lobby, looking around, trying to get a detached perspective on the furnishings. She wondered what the California doctor would think about the decor: unpretentious western-style furniture, colorful Indian rugs scattered on the polished oak floor, and walls of rough logs that matched an open-beam ceiling.

The hotel had been completely renovated and modernized in the last few years without losing its original Old West charm. So far, it had survived the encroaching Colorado ski country development, a sprawl of condominiums and lodges. She didn't know how much longer it would turn a profit. Thank goodness, there were loyal guests who returned every year to Eagle Ridge, and more and more small conferences and seminars were choosing the hotel for their meetings. The hotel's thirty-five rooms were filled every night from May to October.

She had reserved a double room for Steve and his son on the second floor, overlooking the lake. A small balcony gave a panoramic view of the green-carpeted foothills and jagged, snow-tipped peaks. She was certain that he'd find the surroundings spectacular, even if he found the accommodations wanting.

Relax, she schooled herself, her palms moist from nervousness. Even if the attractive doctor preferred more luxurious accommodations, she was almost certain he wouldn't go back on their agreement. During the next four weeks Dr. Sherman would be in and out of the hotel, enjoying a mountain vacation with his son, and at the same time scheduling treatments with Penny. If her daughter made any progress at all, Deanna was determined to arrange for continued sessions with the psychologist when the month was over and he returned to Denver.

Don't expect miracles, she cautioned herself, but germinating hope was there just the same.

IT WAS ALMOST dinnertime when Susan, Penny and an overgrown mutt they called Hobo came bounding into the office. Deanna had hired Susan Whitcomb, a husky seventeen-year-old with a round face and a long pony-tail dangling down her back, to be Penny's companion for the summer. From the beginning, Susan seemed to readily understand Penny's silent communications, and enthusiastically did all the talking for both of them. Deanna sometimes wondered if Susan was making it too easy for Penny not to talk.

Maybe I should ask Dr. Sherman to evaluate the sit-uation, Deanna thought. He would see the interaction between Penny and Susan. Yes, he would be able to suggest ways for Susan to help her. A ripple of relief went through Deanna. How weary she'd become of car-rying the full load of Penny's condition by herself. Now she would have a professional on the spot to share her concerns.

"They're here. At the front desk," Susan bubbled. "Wow, what a hunk! When the guy told Mr. Henderson that he was Steve Sherman, I couldn't believe he was the doctor you've been talking about. More like a model for *Sports Illustrated* magazine, if you ask me. And he's going to be here for a whole month?"

Deanna nodded "He and his son, Travis, will be our guests, and I want everyone to treat them like *guests*." She landed a little heavy on the last word.

"Oh, sure, no problem. Hey, the boy seems like a nice kid. When he patted Hobo, the dog wagged his tail like an egg beater gone berserk. Penny thought it was funny, didn't you, hon?" She laughed down at the little girl who was stroking the dog's shaggy coat of brown fur.

Deanna was relieved to see her daughter's blue eyes were bright and clear, and devoid of the dark shadows that sometimes deepened them to almost black. A good sign.

Deanna stood up, smoothing the folds of her lavender-blue dress, which was fashioned in straight, simple lines that complemented her trim figure. Her legs were firm and shapely, and on impulse, she'd decided to wear high heels just for the smug feeling they gave her. "Well, I guess I'd better say hello."

Susan's eyes sparkled as she took in Deanna's dress and shoes. "Wow, look at you. Gold earrings and everything. You ought to turn a few heads in that outfit...or maybe one in particular. If you know what I mean."

Deanna tried to ignore Susan's broad grin, but she suddenly felt terribly self-conscious. Why on earth had she put on a dress instead of her usual trim slacks and tailored blouse? She shoved aside the glaring truth that her feminine side wanted to impress the California doctor.

"Susan, why don't you take Penny into the dining room, and see what the cook has on the menu for dinner," Deanna said. "You go ahead and order. If Dr. Sherman and Travis haven't eaten, we'll join you in a few minutes."

"Okay, but I tried to see what Maude was preparing and she chased me out before I could find out."

Deanna silently crossed her fingers that the stocky, gray-haired Maude Beaker was as good a cook as she claimed she was. Keeping good help was a constant headache because the resorts nearer the ski areas paid higher wages, and her last cook had quit without notice. Luckily, Maude, apparently an old maid, had come to Red Eagle to live with her nephew, Roy Beaker. She'd told Deanna that Roy was gone all the time, so she'd decided to find work. Deanna couldn't imagine the two of them living together. Roy was as testy as his aunt, and if they ever argued, Deanna feared Maude might decide to move on, leaving Deanna without a cook again. So far, the meals Maude had prepared had been tasty, but nothing fancy. Deanna hoped Steve Sherman wasn't so spoiled by the offerings of chic California hotels and restaurants that his palate rejected plain cooking.

Leaving the dog in the office, Susan and Penny headed for the dining room, and Deanna walked down the hall to the lobby. When she caught sight of Steve standing at the front desk, she knew what had stimulated Susan's adolescent approval. His formfitting jeans and knit shirt could have been on a television commercial showing what sexy men were wearing. He was boyishly handsome with his chestnut hair all windblown, his face tanned from a day in the sun.

"Hi, Mrs. Drake," Travis called before she reached them. He ran over to her and exclaimed, "We're here."

"So you are," she laughed at his exuberance. "Did you have a good trip from Denver?" She really wanted to ask why they were late getting here. She had been anxiously expecting them all day, fearful that something might have gone wrong.

"We saw some big, big elk. A whole bunch. Horns like this." He spread out his arms as far as they would go. "Dad took pictures. We'll show you," he bubbled.

Deanna smiled, "I'd love to see them."

"We even stopped and talked to a bunch of guys who were fishing. They had a whole string of spotted pink fish." He held out his little arms wide to show Deanna how many. "Dad says we're going fishing to catch a bunch of them."

"I said we were going to *try* and catch some," Steve chuckled. "Don't put me on the spot, son."

"There are plenty of trout in the lake," Deanna assured them. "And we even have boats that will take you out in the middle where the big ones are."

"Gosh! Can we do that, Dad?"

"Well, not tonight."

"Tomorrow?"

"Probably not tomorrow." At his son's groan, he smiled. "We don't want to do everything the first day, do we? We'll get everything in, I promise." He knew that his son was walking two feet off the ground, talking and planning all kinds of fun for their mountain vacation. Steve was almost as eager as Travis to enjoy the spectacular Colorado Rockies. He'd been looking forward to spending this vacation time with his son. Combining work with pleasure should work out well for everyone. Scheduling Penny's therapy sessions in the morning would leave the rest of the day for Travis.

"The hotel has a nice playground," Deanna said. "And an indoor swimming pool."

As Steve let his eyes travel to her honey colored hair, lightly tanned skin and blue dress that swirled around a beautiful pair of legs, he could easily picture her in a bathing suit. He chided himself for wondering if she ever swam with the guests.

He picked up the room keys. "First let's get settled in our room."

"I'll have one of the boys take your luggage up, sir," said the desk clerk, a tall, lanky young man with a ready smile.

Deanna was pleased with the way Jeffery Tanner was handling the desk, and hoped Jeffery would stick around awhile, but she knew that as soon as college opened in the fall, he'd be gone. Keeping staff was an ever-present headache.

"I hope you'll find your room satisfactory, Dr. Sherman." Deanna smiled with her usual hostess politeness.

"Steve," he corrected her. "I'm on vacation, remember? And may I call you Deanna? It's a lovely name, by the way. Suits you."

She didn't know quite what he meant by the compliment, but she found her face getting slightly warm under his appreciative gaze. She hoped her voice sounded normal when she suggested, "Why don't you and Travis join us for dinner, Steve? You know Penny, and her nanny, Susan Whitcomb, is with her in the dining room. I don't know what's on the dinner menu, but mountain air usually makes everything taste good."

"Sounds great," Steve responded readily. "Let us freshen up a bit and we'll meet you in the dining room, say, fifteen minutes?"

They made it back downstairs in only ten minutes. Steve had changed into fresh brown slacks and a tan pullover sweater. Travis's face was freshly scrubbed, his hair neatly combed, and he wore a Broncos' sweatshirt that looked brand-new.

Deanna was pleased when Steve looked around the dining room and gave a nod of approval. She had chosen a pastel floral wallpaper and tablecloths in pale green and pink. A series of windows overlooked the lake and mountain valley. A flagstone terrace with potted greenery just outside added to the spacious feeling of the room and made a wonderful setting for early-morning breakfast, midday lunch and evening dinner.

"Very nice," he said. "Warm and inviting."

He smiled at Susan as he took a chair beside her, and Deanna enjoyed a secret smile at the young girl's flustered expression. Travis took a seat on the other side of Susan, and following thoughts of his own, asked, "What's the dog's name?"

"Hobo," answered Deanna.

"That's a funny name," Travis said, frowning.

"It's another word for tramp," Steve explained, and Travis brightened. He'd read a book about a funny tramp who wandered around making people laugh.

"We took Hobo in as a stray, and haven't been able to get rid of his straggly, unkempt look despite brushing and baths," Deanna chuckled. "He seems determined to live up to his name."

"Maybe he would like to be called Prince better, even if he doesn't look like one," Travis offered.

Deanna exchanged an amused look with Steve. She liked his son. Travis was outgoing, smart and full of energy. A wonderful companion for Penny. She said, "I've talked to Susan about looking after Travis when you're busy."

"Great." He'd been wondering who he was going to hire to keep an eye on Travis while he was occupied in the mornings with Penny. "What do you say, Travis? Would you like to keep this pretty girl company some of the time?"

"Sure."

"I can tell we're going to get along great." Susan winked at him, and he winked back.

Deanna was a little on edge when it came time to order, but everyone seemed to find what they wanted on the limited menu, and she began to relax. As they waited for their food, she appreciated how easily Steve handled the conversation. He asked Susan questions about her school and work, smiled at Travis's boyish chatter and addressed remarks to Penny without any apparent notice of her lack of response.

Although Deanna was eager to talk to him about her daughter and show him the playroom, she contained herself until they finished eating dessert, a wonderful deep-dish apple pie that had relieved her worries about the new cook.

When everyone was through eating, she said casually to Susan, "Why don't you take Travis and Penny to the apartment and let them choose one of the movie videos to watch?"

"What kind do you have?" Travis asked bluntly. "All girls' stuff?"

"We have *Lion King,*" Susan said.

He grinned his approval. "My favorite. Come on, Penny. I know all the songs. I'll sing them to you."

Deanna couldn't tell what her daughter was thinking. She seemed to regard Travis with the same interest she had for Hobo when he was chasing his tail. Deanna was a little surprised and relieved when Penny slipped off her chair and left happily with the boy and Susan.

She pushed back her coffee cup, trying to find the right words. Getting off to a good start was very important for the success of this unusual arrangement. "Thank you so very much for coming."

Steve smiled. "No thanks necessary. You have a lovely place here."

"I'm anxious to show you the playroom. I tried to do everything you wanted. If it isn't all right, if I've missed something, or if you want to change anything, just tell me."

A slight tremble in her lower lip betrayed taut nerves, and he hastened to put her at ease. "I'm sure it's fine. Let's just relax tonight." He led the conversation away from her daughter's treatments, and they talked generally about the tourist business.

Deanna began to relax, and when he suggested an after-dinner drink, she nodded. "Yes, I'd like to show you the lounge. I think you'll like the western decor."

As they made their way out of the dining room, several people acknowledged her with a smile, and some of the men seemed to enjoy the way her summer dress complemented her trim figure and long legs. Steve admired the way Deanna carried herself as she walked, gracefully feminine with an air of confidence and purpose. He knew that if they'd met under different circumstances, he would have been interested in knowing her a lot better. Even though it was her daughter who was his patient, and not Deanna, he wanted to keep his interest in this lovely, fascinating woman a professional one.

The lounge was located at the back of the hotel. A colorful sign above a pair of swinging doors read, Rattlesnake Tavern.

Steve read it aloud and looked at Deanna with raised eyebrows. "Just a euphemism, I hope."

She smiled. "Dillon, the bartender, gave the bar that name when my husband was alive. Dillon's been in these parts forever, and the stories he tells are ten percent truth and ninety percent blarney. At least, I hope they're not true," she said with a rather forced laugh.

Uh, oh. Steve's well-trained perception told him that Deanna Drake did not like Dillon. Very interesting. Why did she keep him on? She was the boss, wasn't she? He filed away the question for future notice.

He pushed open the swinging door, and Deanna preceded him into the lounge. The hotel tavern had the ambience of an old western movie. The walls were decorated with horseshoes, lariat ropes, branding irons and other cowboy memorabilia. Pseudo–kerosene lamps with candles in them decorated small round tables and large ceiling wagon-wheel chandeliers hung over a bar that stretched along one wall.

Only about a half-dozen customers sat at the tables and a couple of men had their legs wrapped around stools at the bar. One of them turned around as Steve followed Deanna to a corner table. Out of the corner of his eye, Steve saw him slide off the bar stool and stride purposefully across the room.

When he reached their table, he said, "I see the good doctor has arrived." His bold eyes evaluated Steve as if he was ready to take issue with anything that was said.

"This is Bob Henderson, my hotel manager," Deanna quickly made the introduction. "Dr. Steve Sherman. His son, Travis, is upstairs with Susan and Penny."

Steve stuck out his hand to force a handshake. The snide way the man had landed on the word *good* had alerted Steve. Hostility radiated off the hotel manager like bad fumes, and his handshake was perfunctory.

"I hope you'll find everything to your satisfaction, Doctor. We're not used to having guests who set up practices in our hotel."

Ouch! Steve mentally flinched. This guy wasn't holding back any punches. What gave? Why the icy treatment?

"Bob!" Deanna glared at him. "Dr. Sherman— Steve—is here at my request. He's generous enough to give up some of his vacation time to treat Penny. We want him to enjoy our hospitality—fully."

"Of course, of course," Bob answered mechanically.

"I understand you're planning on being with us a month?" His tone made it clear he considered the visit much too long.

"That's the plan," Steve answered smoothly.

"Deanna's been beside herself trying to get everything ready to your satisfaction." He put a possessive hand on her shoulder and smiled down at her. "Haven't you, honey?"

So that's the way it is. Now Steve understood the hotel manager's hostility. Obviously, he thought Steve's presence might be some kind of personal threat as far as Deanna was concerned. He was ready to declare battle on the big-city doctor who was going to freeload at the hotel for a month.

"Well, I guess I'd better get back to the office. I'm sure you two have a lot to talk about."

"Yes, Bob, we have some scheduling to do and some other details to work out. See you in the morning." Deanna gave him a dismissing smile, while she silently steamed. *How dare he call me honey? And parade his jealousy like some schoolboy?* She struggled to control her anger as he walked away. She wasn't about to create a scene in front of Penny's therapist.

"I don't think Mr. Henderson likes doctors," Steve said after they had ordered their drinks.

"Bob takes a little too much on himself at times," Deanna said in the way of an apology. "But he was a great support when I had all the responsibility of the hotel dumped on me so abruptly."

"I would say that you've done very well. You're to be complimented. It can't be easy running a hotel like this."

"It has its challenges," she said lightly. Keeping her own counsel was one of her strong traits, and she wasn't about to dump a load of frustrations on this willing listener, but suddenly the lounge seemed stifling and confining. "Let's take our drinks out on the terrace. I need a breath of fresh air."

Steve rose and picked up both drinks. As they passed the bar, a craggy-faced man with a black beard wiped his hands on his bartender apron and held out his hand, forcing Steve and Deanna to stop. "You must be the shrink Deanna's been expecting."

"That's me." Steve nodded. "And you must be Dillon, the most famous storyteller in the Rockies." The bartender looked to be about fifty years old, with rawboned features that included a crooked nose and bushy black eyebrows.

"I don't know about the famous part, but I do like to spin a yarn or two," he admitted, stroking his shaggy beard. "Been around Eagle Ridge mostly all my life."

"I'd like to hear some of your stories. I bet there's a lot of interesting history in this area."

"Yep, and plenty of goings-on right today. Nothing much goes on around here that escapes these two eyes of mine. Right, Deanna?"

Her smile was thin. "Everyone loves to come to the Rattlesnake and gossip with Dillon."

"Hey, I'm no gossip. I always check my facts. You better be careful, gal." He shook a stubby finger at her. "Telling tales out of school will only get ya in a peck of trouble."

"And what kind of tales could I tell about you that weren't true?" Deanna countered with quick sharpness.

Dillon gave a grunt that might have passed for a laugh, but then he warned Steve, "Watch out for this gal, Doctor. She's as pretty as a diamondback rattler, and just as dangerous."

Deanna ignored the remark, and Steve saw her face was flushed with anger as they walked away from the bar. A set of double French doors at the back of the lounge led outside to a large terrace bordered by a waist-high rock wall.

Now Steve knew why the tavern was nearly empty. The terrace was filled with hotel guests enjoying their drinks under the stars as they sat at small tables, laughing and chatting. He saw that a four-piece band was setting up at one end of the patio near a small hardwood dance floor.

Deanna eased onto a chair at one of the tables near the low rock wall, and Steve was aware of the deep breath she took as if to settle some disquieting emotion. Obviously the little encounter with the bartender had set her on edge. Even if he hadn't been a professional delving into people's minds and emotions, he would have been intrigued by the double-edged banter that had taken place between them.

"That's Shadow Lake," she said, resuming her conversational tone as she pointed to a wide expanse of water at the base of the hill. "In daytime, the lake is a bright blue, but once the sun goes behind those peaks, the water turns so dark that the shadows of the trees around it are reflected on the surface like black webs."

"Then I'd say its name is appropriate."

"Yes, in more ways than one," she murmured, and then quickly took a sip of her drink.

As Steve looked across the table at her, he was conscious of the way the moonlight played upon her golden hair and traced the lovely lines and planes of her face. If the situation had been different, he could have easily allowed himself to become romantically interested in her, but he was an expert at keeping his love life separate from his profession. He knew how to stay within the bounds of friendship, and even though Deanna Drake intrigued him on more levels than he was willing to admit, he knew how to handle himself. Penny Drake was his patient, and anything that affected her was of vital interest to the success of her treatment.

There was a great deal he needed to learn about Deanna Drake, and the incident that had traumatized her child. He had studied reports sent to him with Penny's referral, and even gone to the library to read news accounts of her husband's murder, but the facts were vague. There had been no clues as to who had shot Benjamin Drake in a small clearing behind the hotel, or why. If Penny knew the answers, they were trapped in her mind, while fear kept close guard, preventing her from speaking them. And if he was successful in releasing the truth? Would the revelations be damaging to Deanna Drake? He was well aware that his first obligation was to his patient, even if the fallout of what he learned from Penny might be critical of her mother.

"Have you always lived in Eagle Ridge?" he asked as they sipped their drinks and drew in the fresh night air.

"No, my parents moved to Colorado when I was twelve. They bought a small ranch in this valley, and I attended a consolidated school about thirty miles from here. After I graduated from high school, I enrolled in a Denver college and took a degree in hotel management. My parents had sold out and moved back East by then, but I decided to stay. Both of them have since passed away. As fate would have it, Ben had posted an assistant manager's job on the college bulletin board. I answered the ad and got the job." Then she added, "And a husband as a fringe benefit."

"Sounds like you two had a lot in common."

She nodded. "Ben was older, had been married when he was in his twenties, and had lost his wife to cancer. He was lonely, and so was I."

"I know how that goes." Steve sighed. "I still miss my wife, Carol. When she died and left me alone with a two-year-old child, I didn't know if I could put my life back together again. Luckily for me, Travis is pure joy." Steve shook his head ruefully and chuckled. "He's a handful sometimes, but he makes life very worthwhile."

"I feel the same way about Penny. Up until now, she's always been such a happy, outgoing little girl—"

"And she will be again," he assured her. He didn't want to talk about Penny, not yet. There would be time later to center the conversation around her child. Because Penny was a minor, he was free to share any insights with her mother as they occurred, and not violate any privileged-information edict that would have governed an adult in his care.

At the moment, he needed to find out as much about Deanna Drake as he could because the child would be affected by whatever was going on in her mother's life. He waited until the right moment seemed to present itself, and then he asked, "Would you satisfy my curiosity about something?"

She smiled at him over the rim of her glass. "Sure. What do you want to know?"

"What's wrong between you and Dillon?"

Her fingers visibly tightened around her drink. She bit her lower lip, and at first he thought she wasn't going to answer. Then she said regretfully, "I wish I knew. When my husband was alive, I had very little to do with the tavern or Dillon. Ben made it clear that he'd handle that part of the hotel, almost as if it were a separate business. Since I've had to take over the management of the hotel, Dillon has shown nothing but antagonism and anger toward me. It's almost…almost as if…as if he believes that I'm the one responsible for Ben's death.''

"I see." He waited for her to go on.

She looked at her drink for a long moment, and then, just as she lifted her eyes to his, they were interrupted by a muscular young man wearing tight jeans and a muscle shirt that showed off his biceps. Steve had noticed the energetic young man with long bleached hair earlier because he'd been helping the musicians set up.

"I know the band's an hour late, Deanna," he said hurriedly. "But it's not my fault. I was in Silver Springs in plenty of time to pick them up and get them here, but the drummer was fooling around with some gal and made us wait. I told them that you'd probably dock their pay."

Deanna shook her head. "Don't worry about it, Roger. I'll settle with them." She motioned to Steve. "I want you to meet Steve Sherman. He's going to be a guest at the hotel for a while. This is Roger. He drives the hotel van and does a little bit of everything else that needs doing around here."

"I used to be a ski instructor at Vail," Roger said quickly to set the record straight. "Had to give it up, though. One of my knees went out and I had to have it replaced. But I'm still in good shape."

Steve almost expected the fellow to flex his muscles to show off his physique. "Yes, I can tell you are."

"Deanna, I need to talk to you about doing some work on the van. It's making noises like the whole differential is about to go out. I was thinking—"

"Tomorrow, Roger," Deanna cut him off. "Tomorrow."

"Oh, sure." He glanced quickly at Steve and then back at Deanna. "Gotcha. Sorry." He gave them a funny kind of salute and left.

Deanna smiled at his retreating back. "Roger's the proverbial jack-of-all-trades and master of none. He showed up last winter looking for a job. He'd be a good mechanic if he'd put his mind to it, or Bob could train him for office work, but he'll never stick with any job very long. I think he was more a ski bum than an instructor in Vail, but his banged-up knee put an end to that life-style."

Steve was sorry that the conversation had turned away from Dillon and whatever it was that made the bartender think Deanna was responsible for her husband's death. He hoped the subject would come up again, but the band started playing and put an end to any easy conversation.

A few couples got up on the dance floor. For a while they just sat, watched and listened, until the barmaid came around to take an order for more drinks.

Deanna shook her head. "I think we'd best be getting upstairs. It's about time to put Penny down for the night, and I imagine Susan has a date. She and Jeffery have been a couple for a few weeks now. Young love, you know," she said in a wistful tone.

"I'd say this is the perfect setting for it." With that said, Steve let his gaze circle the panorama of mountain peaks etched darkly against the night sky.

She didn't answer, and when he turned and looked at her, something in her face touched him in a way he wouldn't have thought possible. Her eyes were filled with such hurt and loneliness that he wanted to pull her close.

He took himself in hand, and as evenly as the sudden quickening of his breath would allow, agreed. "Yes, it's time to turn in. Tomorrow is an important day."

Chapter Three

On the way to her apartment, Deanna asked Steve if he'd like to see the therapy room.

"Tomorrow will be soon enough. I think I'd better collect Travis, and see if I can get him to bed. He's been like a jumping bean all day. I'm afraid he'll wear everyone out with that geyser energy of his."

"He's a darling little boy," Deanna said sincerely. "Penny seems fascinated by him. Believe me, it's been a long time since she's shown interest in any other child. We have a lot of guests who bring their children, and there's a nice playground on the hotel grounds, but Penny won't have anything to do with them." Deanna hesitated and then said, "I guess I ought to warn you that Penny may resist doing anything without the dog nearby."

"No problem. Hobo can come along with her when she comes to the playroom. Actually, using pets in therapy is not uncommon. A lot of kids feel a lot more comfortable with an animal than with a grown-up. Hobo is welcome to try out some of my play therapy." He grinned at her. "We therapists are sneaky guys. We'll use every trick in the book to find success with a child."

She smiled back. "Then I'll relax, knowing that both

my daughter and dog have found a tricky new play-mate.''

As they walked upstairs together, they decided on a daily session from eleven to twelve each morning. Susan would look after Travis for that hour. ''I'll bring Penny up to the therapy room.''

''Good,'' Steve said, and then added that he would meet them at the door because he didn't want her coming into the playroom with Penny. As they entered Deanna's apartment, he explained that it was important to control all the variables during the sessions, and that meant leaving everything else in Penny's life outside the door—except the dog.

The children were sprawled out on the living-room floor, watching the end of the *Lion King* movie, and Susan was curled up on the couch reading a magazine. Both children were sleepy-eyed, and there was no protest when they were told it was time for bed.

''See you tomorrow, Penny. And you, too, Hobo,'' Steve said as he collected Travis and started to leave. The dog wagged his scruffy tail at the sound of his name, but Penny only fixed her flat stare on Steve, and didn't even respond to Travis when he said, '''Night, Penny.''

The room that they'd been assigned was at the opposite wing of the hotel from Deanna's apartment but on the same second floor and almost directly below the therapy room, which was on the third floor.

Travis fell asleep almost the moment he hit the pillow, but Steve lay wide awake, looking out the window, his mind filled with a swirl of thoughts as threatening as the high dark clouds moving across the face of the moon. Maybe this arrangement had been a mistake. Keeping focused on Penny's therapy and not letting himself be drawn into a potentially volatile situation with Deanna would be a challenge. The manager's proprietary manner had clearly been a ''hands off'' warning. What was Deanna's real relationship with Bob Henderson? She'd clearly been annoyed with him. Had he stepped into a lovers' rift? Steve wondered. And if so, what bearing would their relationship have on his stay at the hotel, and more importantly, on his work with Penny?

And what was that undercurrent between her and the bartender, Dillon, all about? Apparently the craggy-faced man had been great friends with Benjamin Drake, and according to Deanna, he held her responsible for Ben's death. Maybe it's a good thing I'm going to stick around awhile, Steve thought. He just might be able to help Deanna handle some of the burden that had landed on her shoulders.

He kneaded his pillow, flounced over in bed and lectured himself about the protective urges that he was feeling for this woman he'd just met.

THE NEXT MORNING, Steve stood waiting in the open doorway of the therapy room when Deanna and Penny came up the stairs with Hobo bounding ahead of them. Whether or not the little girl would come willingly into the room without her mother was the first hurdle. Sometimes a child resisted being left alone with the therapist and the first few sessions were unproductive. Nevertheless, Steve was always firm about making the child adjust to being without any parent during therapy.

He was relieved when Penny showed no hesitancy about coming into the playroom with her dog for a look-see. He suspected that Penny must have overheard some of Deanna's preparations for furnishing the therapy room and was curious about it.

Steve gave Deanna the "okay" sign, and then shut the door. The little girl didn't seem to notice or be concerned that her mother had gone. Shiny golden curls framed her solemn face, and a shower of freckles dotted her slightly pug nose. She would have been a beautiful child if there'd been a bit of life in her vacant expression.

Steve released a thankful breath that she hadn't shown any resistance to staying in the playroom. He made himself comfortable on a floor cushion beside a low round table like the one he had in his office. Sitting quietly, he watched the child and dog explore the room.

Hobo sniffed at everything, poked his nose into buckets of toys, and accidentally set a ball rolling with his nose. Penny slowly made a circuit of the room, looking at the dollhouse, sandbox, an easel set up with paper, crayon and paints and an array of puppets and stuffed animals sitting on a shelf, but she didn't touch anything.

Apparently having satisfied her curiosity, she started toward the door and motioned for Hobo to follow. She was ready to leave.

"Penny."

She stopped and looked at Steve, her eyes fixed and staring.

He held up a small kitchen timer that was ticking away. "Have you seen a timer, Penny? Like this one? Your mother wants you to stay until this hand goes all the way around. That's an hour. You can do anything you want until the bell dings. Anything at all. You can play or not play. It's up to you, but you have to stay here until it's time to go."

She looked at him, at the timer, and then at the closed

door. Her expression remained the same, closed and guarded. No sign of tears, nor hysterics, nor hint of any kind of emotion.

Hobo came over to the low table where Steve was sitting and sniffed at a plastic bag of cookies that he had requested from Maude, the cook.

"I know what Hobo wants." Steve laughed and held up the sack. "He wants to eat a cookie. Do you want to give him one?"

There was no visible response on her face, but as Hobo did some dancing turns, begging for the cookie, Penny slowly moved closer to the table.

As Steve held out the sack to her, the dog poked at it with his nose, drooling with anticipation. "Do you want to give Hobo a cookie?"

Without even a responding flicker of her eyelashes, she took the sack, pulled out a cookie and gave it to Hobo. Then she handed the sack back to Steve.

"Does Penny want a cookie?"

As if she hadn't heard him, the little girl's eyes flickered to the closed door and back again.

The first hurdle had come.

Steve kept his smile relaxed as she just stood there. Would Penny accept the time allotment? Or would she challenge his authority to keep her in the playroom? Would she waste precious time in tantrums as some children did?

He waited. The only sound in the room was the ticking of the timer and Hobo's chomping down his cookie. After a moment, Penny lowered her head, fixed her eyes on the floor and just stood there. She looked so small, alone and vulnerable that it was all he could do not to reach a hand out to her, but he knew that building the child's inner strength could not be imposed from the outside. Deanna's love would have healed the little girl if tender caring was all that was needed.

"For the time we have together, Penny, you can do just as you please. If there's something you want to play with, you can. But if you don't want to play, you don't have to," he assured her again.

Slowly Penny lifted her eyes from the floor, looked at the door and then back to him. Then she let her gaze go around the room.

Steve breathed a silent *Good girl.* He couldn't direct the little girl or make any suggestions. For the hour she spent with him each day, Penny had to feel perfectly free to do whatever interested her, or to do nothing at all. All he could do was provide a safe environment so she would feel free to express the dark forces that kept her withdrawn. The traumatic blockage that made her fearful of being herself had to be removed, and only when he knew what that was could he help her back to normalcy. He pretended interest in making notes in a small notebook, wondering how long she would stand there.

Very slowly Penny began walking around the room. Once again she passed over all the toys and equipment without touching anything. Out of the corner of his eye, Steve saw her stop in front of a large window overlooking the grounds below. With purposeful deliberation, she pulled the cord that closed the drapes, shutting out the bright sunlight. Then she walked over to a small exercise mat in one corner of the room and lay on it. When Hobo came over to sniff at her, she pulled him down beside her.

Steve made the proper notes for his record, then he stretched his long legs out in front of him and waited to see what she would do next.

Nothing.

Penny lay there, staring at the ceiling for a long time. The hour passed and when the timer rang both Penny and her dog were asleep.

The dog lifted his head as Steve came over to the mat and sat beside the sleeping child. "Time to wake up, Penny."

Long eyelashes fringing her pale cheeks lifted slowly. For a moment, Penny's eyes were clear, but instantly darkened with shadows as she sat up.

"You had a nice nap," Steve said reassuringly. "And so did Hobo.

Flushed with sleep, Penny rubbed her eyes, and at that moment she looked soft and cuddly. The child had inherited the same fine cameo features as her mother, and the same hint of natural curl in her corn-silk hair. No doubt Penny had inherited her mother's strong will as well. Deanna had said that her daughter was a vivacious and outgoing child before the night her father was murdered.

The personality change was an effect of the trauma, and Steve knew that Penny's withdrawal was a protective instinct, a barricade against frightening circumstances. How soon she would be willing to lower it would depend in great part upon how quickly she would trust him.

"It's time for lunch. Are you hungry?"

No response.

"We'll shut up the playroom until tomorrow. This is yours and Hobo's place—no one else's."

Penny got up and walked slowly to the door. Then she stood there waiting for Steve to open it. When he turned the knob, showing that it wasn't locked, he knew from the almost imperceptible flicker of her eyelids that she was surprised. Would the little girl have stayed if she'd known she could turn the knob and walk out?

Deanna was waiting for them in the hall, and for the last ten minutes she'd been looking at her watch, wondering what was going on inside that room. As they came out, she couldn't tell from Steve's face whether things had gone well or not, but he laughed as Penny and Hobo bounded down the stairs, so she took that to be a good sign.

Her smile held an unspoken, "Well?"

"Everything went fine." That's all Steve was going to say at the moment. As he'd explained to Deanna before, he never discussed with parents the specifics of what went on during therapy unless he felt he needed some more information that parents could supply, or it was time to share something with them that had a bearing on the child's continued progress. A casual remark made by a parent could easily destroy the trust the child was building in the therapist.

Steve doubted that Deanna would be able to appreciate the importance of Penny's nonresistance to staying in the room. Until a child was willing to stay an hour in the room, there was little chance of success using play therapy. She had no idea how long and fierce that battle could be.

Deanna translated his noncommittal answer—he really wasn't going to talk about the sessions, at least not now. It wouldn't be easy to curb her desire to know everything that was happening to her child, but she would have to trust him to tell her the things she should know. Deanna was determined not to be one of those anxious parents who put a doctor through the third degree every chance they got.

"What are your plans for the rest of the day?" she asked in her hotel-activities director's voice.

"Any suggestions?" he asked in the same light tone.

"Well, there's the hotel swimming pool, boating and fishing on the lake, and a lot of hiking trails. I guess I should warn you, Travis found out there's a riding stable near here and he's gearing up for a horseback ride this afternoon."

"Ouch," Steve said in mock pain. "I remember the last horseback ride I took. Believe me, the horse and I didn't part the best of friends."

"The riding stable has lots of easy-riding horses and guides. You could start out with a short ride up to Chimney Rock," she told him. "It's a gentle climb and you can see most of the mountain valley from there. The view might give you a better idea of the fishing streams, as well as some possible camping places and available horseback-riding trails. You shouldn't have any trouble filling up your vacation. Everything for the outdoor man is right here."

"You mean, the outdoor boy, don't you? It's that son of mine who wants to play mountain man."

She laughed in agreement. "Travis has been poring over some maps and brochures while you were with Penny. He's especially excited about our guided horseback trips into the wilderness areas."

Steve groaned.

"Are you telling me you're out of condition?" she chided.

"No, I'm telling you I prefer a racquetball court to climbing mountains."

"Too bad. We don't have any racquetball courts, but we have plenty of mountains."

"How about taking a walk around Shadow Lake this

afternoon? You could show us some of the points of interest.''

''Sorry, I have a meeting scheduled with a group who want to reserve the hotel for a conference. I'll be busy the rest of today and tomorrow.''

And the day after that? In a way Steve was relieved that she was making it clear that she wasn't going to step over any line that would put their relationship on anything but a professional basis. The more he was around Deanna Drake, the challenge of resisting the growing attraction he felt for her was demanding more and more willpower.

''Well, I think Travis and I will take that hike he's been wanting, and then spend some time in the swimming pool. We'll save the boating for another day.''

HE WAS GRATEFUL that he'd made a deal with Susan to include Travis in her child-care duties. After he and Travis had come back from their hike and spent an hour in the pool, Susan took both children out to the playground.

Steve wandered around the hotel at his leisure, keeping his eye out for Deanna. When he found her, she was outside in the hotel parking lot, talking to Roger, the ex–ski bum. They were in the middle of a discussion about the ailing hotel van.

''All right, call Denver and have the part sent up by express,'' Deanna was saying. ''In the meantime, you can use the Subaru for errands. Are you sure you know what's wrong with the van?''

''Am I sure?'' Roger grabbed his chest in mock pain. ''How can you doubt the best mechanic this side of the continental divide?''

"Because you're full of the blarney and you know it."

Roger winked at Steve. "She loves me."

"Don't flatter yourself." Deanna gave the cocky young man a playful shove. "Go on, order the part. Maude's going to have a fit if you don't start getting her orders to the kitchen on time."

"That battle-ax."

"She's the only cook I've got, and I'll string you up by your thumbs if you make her quit."

He gave Deanna a salute. "Yes, ma'am." As he walked away, muscles rippled in his back and thighs, but Steve noticed he favored one leg. Probably the knee he'd hurt skiing.

"Seems like a nice kid."

"He's no kid. He's twenty-eight or nine. Anyway, he's been hanging around Eagle Ridge for quite a while. Ben depended upon him to be the hotel gofer." She sighed. "This has been one of those days that validate the principle that if something can go wrong, it will."

Steve decided that Deanna looked like a gal who needed a break. "How about a glass of lemonade or something stronger?"

"Lemonade sounds good." For some foolish reason, Deanna's spirits instantly lifted, and she wished she'd had time to freshen up a bit. He'd been in her thoughts off and on all afternoon, and several times she'd made some mistakes that were the result of her daydreaming.

The dining room was nearly empty when they took a seat by the window and ordered a pitcher of lemonade and some sugar cookies. Deanna was just beginning to relax, when Murphy's Law lived up to its reputation, and her rising spirits took another nosedive.

When Sheriff Janson glanced in the dining room, she

knew that he'd come looking for her. "Not today," she breathed a protest as he came in.

Steve followed her look and asked, "Who is it?"

"Sheriff Janson."

Steve thought the burly, potbellied man in tight western pants and shirt looked more like a ranch boss than a law officer. He wore a dark cowboy hat perched on the back of his head, and tufts of graying eyebrows hung over dark eyes that were as sharp as polished iron.

Deanna's stomach tightened as she put down her half-eaten cookie. Sheriff Janson had made it clear from the beginning of his investigation into Ben's death that she was high on his list of suspects.

"Sorry to intrude on you folks," he said with little sign that he really meant the apology. Taking off his hat, he held out a gnarled hand to Steve. "Sheriff Janson. I reckon you're the fellow fixing to help Penny get over her dark spell. Sherman, isn't it?"

"Dr. Steve Sherman. Glad to meet you." Usually Steve didn't bother with the doctor moniker, but Deanna's reaction to the man had put him on guard. Suddenly she was sitting with her spine pressed against the back of her chair like a cornered animal, every muscle ready for flight. He couldn't quite tell what was going on between Deanna and the sheriff, but the air was filled with some unspoken hostility. Why was she reacting so negatively to a law officer who must be trying to find her husband's killer?

"Well, now, Doc, I sure hope things work out with Penny. The little tyke just might have the answer to all of this. I'll be checking in to find out what she has to say."

Steve started to enlighten the sheriff about doctor-patient confidentiality, but decided the time wasn't right. He'd wait until Janson started pushing him, and then he'd set the record straight.

"I guess you haven't turned up anything new in your investigation, Sheriff," she said, "otherwise you wouldn't still be hanging around the hotel."

The tone and manner of her remark verified Steve's thoughts. *No love lost between the two of them.*

"Well, now." Janson scratched his head, still standing by the table. Steve noticed that Deanna had not asked him to sit down. "Sometimes a body can learn a lot just listening to folks flap their gums a bit. Take Dillon, for instance. I'll admit he can go off the deep end sometimes, but a bartender sees and hears things that can set him to thinking—"

"In the wrong direction," she raged.

The sheriff's bushy eyebrows matted thoughtfully over the bridge of his nose as he peered at Deanna for a long moment. He shook his head when the waitress came up and asked if he would like to order something. Then he said, "Oh, no, I don't want to intrude on this little party."

Deanna swallowed hard to keep from retorting that he already had. The sheriff stuck his hat on the back of his head. "Well, I'll be moseying along. Guess I'll hit Dillon up for a beer. Nice to meet you, Doc. We'll have to have a talk real soon."

"Yes, I'd like that," Steve responded readily. People intrigued him. All kinds of people. Now he had two interesting good old boys to put under his professional microscope, and if both Dillon and Janson were lined up against Deanna, maybe he could even the sides.

"Sorry about that," Deanna apologized.

"Don't be. Maybe if I understood the situation a little better, I might be of some help to you."

He watched as she struggled to make the decision whether or not to confide in him. He knew well enough that unless a situation impacted Penny in some way, he had no right to involve himself in it. Deanna was not his patient. Any help he gave her would be on a personal basis, friend to friend.

"It's a sordid mess."

He only nodded and waited.

She worried the napkin in her hand for a moment, then the decision made, she lifted her head and met his eyes. "Dillon has been filling Janson's ears with a lot of half truths about me and Bob Henderson, a sordid tale that would make good tabloid copy. 'Lovers Kill Husband for Hotel.'"

Steve was adept at not showing any emotion to whatever was said. He just nodded to show he accepted what she was telling him. "Dillon has made a deal with me. He won't go to the newspapers with his suspicions if I let him go on running the bar."

That's blackmail, pure and simple.

Her voice was flat and resigned as she echoed his thought. "I know I shouldn't let him blackmail me, but at the moment my first consideration is Penny. There was some publicity in the beginning when Ben was shot, but, thank God, it died down when the police hit a dead end. Dillon could stir everything up again. I don't want the news media latching on to the story, slapping Penny's picture all over the place, and capitalizing on her trauma. Don't you see that I really have no choice but to go along with Dillon, hoping that he'll keep the lies to himself as long as I employ him?"

Steve wanted to tell her to call the bartender's bluff. His temper flared just thinking about the way the unscrupulous man was using her, but he knew she was right. The tabloids would eat up this kind of story. Even if Dillon put out a bunch of lies, the damage would be done. The scenario was a familiar one. Anyone with two eyes in his head could see that Bob Henderson had feelings for Deanna Drake. Steve wondered once again if they were having an affair, or had been lovers in the past, but he knew that he'd have to let the answer come from her. He had no right to pry into her personal life unless it became evident that there was something he needed to know for her daughter's sake. There was a fine line between his professional obligations and a personal interest in knowing about Deanna Drake's love life.

"Maybe when Penny tells us what she knows we'll have some answers," she said hopefully.

"And maybe not." Steve didn't want to encourage any wishful thinking. "Even if we overcome the effects of the trauma, Penny's memory may not provide us with any significant details. We'll have to wait and see."

"Yes, of course." She drew in a breath. "Thanks for keeping me focused."

"You've been carrying a heavy load all by yourself, haven't you?"

She nodded. "You don't know how grateful I am that you're willing to work with Penny. I'll do anything to get my happy chatterbox back again." She quickly turned away, and he suspected she hid eyes filled with tears.

Because of his own child, compassion for her heartache touched Steve and he fought an urge to reach over and take her hand. He had known from the first moment he saw her that she was a strong, determined woman, but he was only now beginning to glimpse how courageous she was.

"What kind of a sheriff is this guy Janson? Is he a good lawman?"

"On the whole, I'd say he's as good as most sheriffs are. Tenacious. Stubborn. He's like a bloodhound—only this time he's following the wrong scent." Her chin hardened. "I think Dillon's just about convinced him that somewhere there's proof I shot Ben." The cords in her lovely neck tightened. "And your obvious next question, Doctor—is there proof?"

"Is there?"

"No, but I don't blamc you if you want to pack up and leave now that you know the situation."

Do I really know the situation?

Deanna saw the question in his eyes, and turned away from it. How could she reassure him of anything? She'd searched every memory until it was threadbare, trying to find a rhyme or reason for what had happened.

Where had the horror begun?

And where would it end?

Chapter Four

Steve saw little of Deanna the next few days, and his sessions with Penny settled into a pattern. While Hobo bounded around the playroom, sniffing and wagging his scrawny tail, Penny wandered around listlessly, looking at everything but showing no desire to draw pictures or play in the sandbox or dollhouse.

Steve made certain that everything was in the same place every day. One of the hotel maids was careless about her cleaning, and was inclined to shove things around as she dusted and swept the floor, but Steve wanted the environment in the therapy room to be secure and unchanged.

Every day, after a few minutes of looking around, Penny walked over to the window, drew the drapes and then dropped onto the corner floor mat. Sometimes she would lie on her back and, with her eyes wide open, stare at the ceiling. Sometimes she would turn over on her side and watch Hobo as he snooped around the room. The dog was always interested in the snacks that Steve had ready on the low table, and pestered him for food.

"You like cookies, don't you, Hobo?" When Steve

spoke to him and patted his head, Hobo's tail wagged as if it were going to drop off from excitement.

Knowing that Penny was watching, one morning Steve rolled a ball across the room and Hobo brought it back. They played fetch for several minutes, and Steve didn't make any effort to include Penny in the game. In play therapy, the child made all the choices, and as frustrating as it might be, nothing could be gained by imposing choices upon Penny.

At the end of the first week of sessions, Penny still remained passive and hadn't shown the slightest interest in anything in the playroom. He gave his usual smile to Deanna as she collected the child and dog, without giving any sign of the lack of progress he was making with her daughter.

He sighed as he opened the window drapes that Penny habitually closed. When he heard light footsteps just outside the open hall door a few minutes after Deanna had left with her daughter, he turned and saw that she was standing in the doorway.

"Hi. Can I come in?"

"Sure. We've closed up shop for the weekend."

It was the first time since his arrival at the hotel that she'd come anywhere near the playroom, and lately, every time he saw her around the hotel, she was too busy to do much chatting. "Want a cookie?"

She laughed and shook her head. "I just popped in for a minute, in case you wanted to tell me anything about…about the way Penny is responding."

"I'm not sure I know how she's responding. Not yet. Maybe you could clarify a few things for me?"

She nodded. "What would you like to know?"

"Does Penny seem to feel more comfortable in

closed-in places with dim light and the window blinds drawn?''

Deanna looked puzzled. ''Not at all. Where did you get that idea?''

''She doesn't prefer the window drapes drawn in her room?''

Deanna shook her head. ''Heavens no. Penny has a window seat in her bedroom and plays there all the time. Our whole apartment is light and airy. I don't understand what you're getting at.''

Steve motioned her over to the window. ''Every day Penny draws the drapes on this window. I thought she was shutting out the light.''

Deanna looked out the third-story window, which overlooked a wooded area covered with white-trunk aspen and tall ponderosa pine trees. She swallowed hard is if there was a sudden catch in her throat.

''What is it?'' Steve asked, concerned that her face had suddenly gone ashen.

''It's not the light she's shutting out.''

''What then?'' Steve touched her arm. ''I need to know,'' he said quietly.

She moistened her lips. ''Down there...in those trees...that's where they found the body of my husband.''

Deanna's composure crumbled in front of his eyes, and for a moment Steve's professional training almost deserted him. He wanted to pull her close, comfort her and ease the emotional load she was carrying. He knew he should calmly pattern back the words she'd spoken, *That's where they found the body of your husband,* but his voice was lost somewhere in his chest. Before he could say anything, she turned and walked away from him.

"Choosing this room was a mistake. I'm sorry. Penny's bedroom used to be on this side of the hotel. After Ben's death, we moved to a different apartment in another wing. When I chose this room for therapy, I didn't think about it overlooking the wooded area. It's my fault. I should have anticipated something like this."

"Hey, I'm glad to know the reason for Penny's behavior. Don't beat yourself up. Obviously the view from the window is something she wants to shut out."

Deanna nodded. "I feel stupid for not thinking about it. This was the room with the most floor space."

"No harm done, but it's obvious that we'll have to change rooms."

"Yes, of course." She took a deep breath and let her managerial skills take over as she quickly reviewed in her mind all the other rooms that might be suitable. Most of the regular rooms were too small to accommodate all of the things Steve had requested for the playroom. The only other accommodation was a spacious room overlooking the front grounds of the hotel that would work nicely if they emptied it of the furnishings. She knew that Bob would have a fit forfeiting a month's rental on the deluxe room, but she felt that it was more important not to lose any more time. No telling when Steve would decide that this "on-location" therapy wasn't working. She'd seen his expression when she'd told him why Penny was closing off the window, and at that moment, she felt like someone trapped in a collapsing building, waiting for the timbers to fall.

"Is moving going to be a problem?" he asked as he watched worry mirrored in her eyes.

"No, not at all," she said hurriedly. "There's a room

on the third floor, at the front of the building, that should work. Why don't you have a look at it, and if you think it's satisfactory, I'll arrange to have the move made this afternoon.''

"Fine.'' He followed as Deanna led the way.

When Steve saw the room, he knew it was obviously one of the hotel's best accommodations, and he couldn't help wondering what giving up the rental was going to cost her. He had already decided that he was going to pay for his and Travis's room, even though the agreement had been that they would be her guests for the month of June. He knew she'd put up an argument when he waived his fee.

"What do you think?'' she asked anxiously.

"This is very nice,'' he said, "but since we are going to have to make a change, a smaller room might be okay. We could make do with less floor space and—''

"No. Our deal was that I would provide a complete therapy room for Penny's treatment. We've already had one setback. I'm going to make certain there isn't another one.''

"Hey, quit tearing yourself up.'' He gave her a reassuring smile. "Nothing's been lost. In fact, we may have gained something.''

"Are you sure?'' Hope and relief flickered in her eyes.

"Positive. If you don't mind, I'd like to make another suggestion. So far, the only time I've had a chance to see Penny outside of the therapy room was at dinner the night we arrived. It might be a help to me if I could see Penny in a regular setting now and again.''

She looked puzzled. "What did you have in mind?''

"I know you're terribly busy, but I was wondering

if, perhaps, we could all do something together? Penny, Travis, you and I?''

''Like what?'' She wasn't exactly sure what he was suggesting. Did he want to set up a situation strictly for observation, or was he feeling her out about spending some personal time with him and his son? She wanted to be sure of her ground before making a fool of herself by eagerly agreeing to broaden any contact between them.

''How about that picnic by the lake that you talked about?'' The twinkle in his eyes told her he wasn't talking about any clinical observation, but an afternoon of fun for all of them. ''As far as I can tell, your workload is out of balance with your leisure time. You ought to lighten up a bit.'' He winked at her. ''Doctor's orders.''

''Well, in that case, Doctor, a picnic it is,'' she agreed, and her low spirits suddenly dropped away. ''I'll talk to Maude about a picnic lunch. Say, one o'clock?''

''It's a date.''

Deanna couldn't believe that she was actually humming as she went downstairs to give orders for switching furniture in the two rooms. Her days were spent making sure her guests had a good time. It had been a long time since she'd spent any time relaxing at the lake. And somehow, Steve had made her feel that everything was under control.

Unfortunately, her high spirits were dashed with cold water when she entered the kitchen. She saw Sheriff Janson in deep conversation with Maude, who was chopping vegetables at a salad table. From their expressions and the abrupt way they stopped talking, Deanna guessed that she must have been the topic of conversation.

"Howdy," the sheriff greeted her with his usual affability. "Don't you look prettier than a prairie flower today, Deanna. You've got more color in your cheeks than I've seen for a long time."

The compliment had a double edge to it. She knew he was digging for the reason, so she smiled sweetly. "Thanks. I've decided to spend a little time relaxing today. Maude, will you fix me up a picnic basket? Sandwiches will be fine, enough for four."

"How soon you want it?" Maude asked in her gruff voice. The husky woman would never win any personality awards, but she'd turned out to be a good worker. Deanna was afraid Maude's wandering nephew would come back and the independent old gal would up and leave Eagle Ridge if she didn't like living with him. Deanna couldn't even begin to think about trying to find another cook.

She had an uneasy feeling about Maude Beaker and the sheriff spending time together. Was Janson lining up some of the hotel staff to keep an eye on her? No doubt he was looking for confirmation that she and Bob were romantically involved. Dillon had done a good job seeding the suspicion that they were accomplices in her husband's death.

"Can you have the basket ready about one o'clock?" Deanna asked.

"Sounds like kind of a party. Who's going with you and Penny?" the sheriff asked in his nosy way.

"Dr. Sherman and Travis."

"Not Bob."

"No, not Bob."

"Hmm, I see."

"I'm not sure you do, Sheriff," Deanna replied

sweetly, turned and left the kitchen, muttering under her breath.

MAUDE HAD the lunch basket ready on time and filled to the top with food and drink. When Steve and Travis joined Penny and her, she saw that Steve had changed into jeans and a knit pullover. He had two fishing poles in his hands and a fishing basket hanging over one shoulder. She smiled to herself. He looked for all the world like an advertisement for *Outdoor Magazine*.

"I thought Travis and I might do a little fishing," he said when he caught a glimpse of a smile tugging on the corner of her mouth.

"Good idea." Her grin spread. "We'll see what kind of fishermen you are. We can walk around to the far end of the lake for our picnic. You might have good luck reeling in a few trout at that spot where a mountain stream feeds into the lake."

As they left the hotel, she chided herself for the quiver of pleasure that his company gave her. Lifting her face to a caressing pine scented breeze, she breathed in deeply and an invisible weight seemed to slip off her shoulders. A glorious deep blue sky was dotted with whorls of white clouds dancing over craggy Rocky Mountain peaks, and her very soul expanded at the wonder of it all.

With Hobo bouncing ahead, they followed a path through stands of white-trunked aspen trees and tall ponderosa pines. Penny seemed willing enough to walk silently beside Travis as he chattered enthusiastically about blue jays flashing their bright blue feathers in the needle branches.

When he stopped to gather up some pinecones, Penny watched, but made no effort to join him, and when

Travis offered the little girl a couple of pinecones, she just looked at them in his hand.

Deanna's heart tightened, remembering how her child had once darted about, piling up pinecones with joyful squeals of laughter. She almost shouted with joy when Penny reached out and took the two cones from Travis's hand. A surge of new hope made her laugh aloud.

Her laughter was full and deep, and the way her eyes glistened with sudden animation took Steve by surprise. Her lips softened in appealing lines that made him entertain an unprofessional impulse to take this beautiful, vivacious woman in his arms. Beyond words and alive with promise, the shared moment arched between them. Their eyes held for a long moment before both of them looked away quickly. They fell silent as they walked together in a suspended awareness that made them both totally conscious of each other.

The path they followed skirted the edge of the lake, and they could see people in small boats trolling fishing lines. Travis immediately started begging, "Can't we get a boat? Please, Dad, please."

"Not today," he said gently but firmly. Then he directed Travis's and Penny's attention to a bushy tail squirrel scurrying along the ground like someone late for an appointment.

A good father, thought Deanna. *Generous but firm.* She wondered what his wife had been like. Anyone could tell by the way he talked about her that he'd been totally in love with her. The fact that a good-looking, personable man like himself hadn't married again was evidence that no other woman could measure up to the love he'd lost. Deanna entertained a moment of discontent that was at odds with the pleasant outing.

They spread their picnic on a grassy knoll overlooking the lake. Maude had ignored Deanna's suggestion of sandwiches and had packed cold fried chicken, small tubs of potato salad and mixed fruit, cookies and a thermos of lemonade.

"Delicious," Steve said, licking his fingers after enjoying a moist, well-seasoned chicken breast.

Neither of the children ate much. Travis was in a hurry to try fishing, and Penny's interest in food was never very high. Steve resisted his son's excited pleas to hurry, and told him to be patient. "We have the whole afternoon to try our luck."

"Can I skip rocks across the water the way you showed me?"

"Sure, go ahead. Just stay out of the water."

"Come on, Penny." Travis waved a hand toward the lake. "You can help me find some small flat stones."

Penny didn't respond to the invitation. Hobo was the one who bounded up eagerly, ready to go. As Travis took off toward the edge of the lake, the dog at his heels, Penny watched for a moment, then she got to her feet and trailed after them.

"Hurrah for Hobo." Steve nodded in satisfaction. "For the moment, he's Penny's security blanket. Is he a new pet or have you had him a long time?"

"We got him right after Ben was killed, when Penny withdrew from everything. We'd never had a dog before, and one day Hobo showed up at the kitchen. I suspect that somebody left him behind when they moved. There's a lot of that in these mountain communities. Anyway, at first, Penny ignored the dog like she does everyone else, but little by little Hobo became her only playmate."

"Sometimes pets can be the truest friend a kid can have."

"Are you a dog person?"

"Not really. When I was growing up, we moved a lot, and after I was married, Carol and I did a lot of traveling. It didn't seem fair to keep a dog in the kennel all the time. I think Carol was more of a cat person, anyway. She loved kittens. And kids."

"You were lucky to marry someone like that."

The wistful edge to her voice made him ask, "Were you and Ben planning on having more children?"

"No." She shook her head sadly. She broke off a blade of squirrel grass and chewed thoughtfully on it. "Ben felt he was too old to be raising a family. He tried his best to relate to Penny, and in his own way he was a good father. I mean, he was willing to give her everything she needed."

Steve waited, knowing that she needed to put some of her thoughts into words.

"Ben gave me security. I was raised dirt poor. My folks never had anything more than the necessities. I put myself through business college, and when I came to work for Ben, I wanted more than anything to belong somewhere."

"So you married him."

"Yes, but we were never really close, not the way you and Carol must have been. More a marriage of convenience, I guess you'd say. I didn't realize how much I didn't know about Ben until he was killed. The sheriff thinks I'm trying to protect his reputation by hiding something, but I'm not. Ben never confided in me about his business dealings. I have no idea why someone would want to kill him. You believe me, don't you?"

Up until that point, Steve had not dismissed the possibility that she was involved in a cover-up of some kind, and was surprised at the conviction in his own words as he answered, "I believe you."

Her eyes were moist as she smiled at him, and he forced himself to say, "I guess I'd better get those fishing lines in the water. Travis isn't going to be patient much longer."

She nodded. "Thank you for listening."

"That's what I do best" He stood up, then reached down a hand and pulled her to her feet. In a bold act he didn't quite understand, he held her hand all the way down to the lake.

Steve threw out the first fishing line, and it went *plunk* only a few feet out into the water. Deanna covered her mouth, trying not to laugh.

Steve saw her mirth and conceded. "I don't quite have the hang of it."

"No, I'm afraid you don't."

"You think you can do better?"

"Travis could probably do better," she teased. "I can tell you're used to deep-sea fishing where you just drop a hook into the water and a moving boat does the rest."

"Guilty as charged. What do you suggest?"

"It's all in the wrist. Like this." She took the pole from him. After whipping the line slightly behind her, she cast it forward into the air in a high arch, letting the baited hook fall yards out into the lake.

As he watched her, his senses were bombarded with the grace and beauty of her body as she captured the sweep and lifting spin of the fishing line. Something deep within his spirit took flight just looking at her.

"See?"

He jerked his thoughts away from dangerous shoals, and tried to pay attention to what she was saying.

"Now you try it."

He did his best, but he only managed to drop the line about half the distance from hers.

"It comes with practice," she said kindly.

All this time, Travis had been holding the first pole that Deanna had thrown out. Suddenly he squealed and began dancing as the reel on his pole began to spin out. "I got one. I got one."

Deanna quickly moved to his side as his fishing pole dipped from the force of the fighting fish. With her help, he reeled in a twelve-inch rainbow trout. As it flopped about on the ground, Hobo ran around in circles barking, while Steve and Deanna slapped Travis on the back and pronounced him a champion fisherman. Penny even held open the fishing basket so he could drop in his prize.

As Steve and Travis settled in for an afternoon of fishing, Deanna was content to lie back on the ground with Penny, and point out cloud pictures as they formed and moved against the blue sky. A sleepy Penny curled up with Hobo for her afternoon nap.

Deanna relaxed, and she wasn't quite sure whether she had fallen asleep or just closed her eyes, when suddenly she was aware of someone standing over her. She blinked to put the figure in focus.

Bob Henderson's round face stared down at her. Hobo bounded to his feet, and both Deanna and Penny sat up. "So there you are, sleeping on the job," he said ungraciously. "Maude told me you were off on a picnic."

Deanna tried to keep the irritation out of her voice. "What is it, Bob?"

"You had a noon date with a committee of international lawyers who are looking over the hotel for their upcoming conference. Did you forget?"

She groaned. "I did."

"I thought so," he said with irritated satisfaction. "I couldn't believe it when all these people arrived, and you were nowhere to be seen."

"I didn't check my day calendar this morning. I got sidetracked with changing Penny's therapy room."

"Changing rooms? What are you talking about?" He frowned. "What was the matter with the room you fixed up? Wasn't it good enough for the city doctor?"

"There were problems," Deanna said evasively.

From a distance, Steve couldn't tell what the heated conversation was about between Deanna and Bob Henderson, but he pulled in his fishing line, put down the pole and walked over to them. One look at Deanna's unhappy expression and he asked, "Is something wrong?"

"I have to get back to the hotel," she said bluntly. "I forgot an important meeting."

Bob's smile edged on smugness. "Sorry to break up the party, folks."

Yeah, sure you are, Steve thought. Bob Henderson's smiling, affable manner went about skin deep, and his no-trespassing attitude where Deanna was concerned was as loud as a brass band. If it hadn't been the meeting, Steve was convinced that the guy would have found something else to scuttle the afternoon outing.

Deanna sighed. "Come on, Penny. We have to go back to the hotel now." She held out her hand to her daughter, but Penny was looking at Travis who was still standing at the lake's edge, throwing his line into the water.

"Would you like to stay and fish with Travis?" Steve asked, hoping that the child might be developing enough confidence to move out a little on her own.

His hope was premature.

Penny didn't even acknowledge Steve's invitation. Without looking at him, she took her mother's hand, and with the other one motioned for Hobo to follow.

Steve followed with his eyes as they walked away. Penny was between her mother and Bob, the three of them looking for all the world like a family unit. Steve didn't like the uneasy feeling that came over him. Was there any merit to Dillon's gossip that there had been— or still was—a romantic liaison between Deanna and her hotel manager?

"Maybe I ought to have a nightcap in the bar and have a chat with the bartender," Steve told himself. Dillon seemed convinced that the two of them were romantically involved. And if they were, Steve wanted to know if their affair began before, or after, her husband was killed.

AFTER TRAVIS had been tucked in for the night, knowing his son wouldn't stir until morning, Steve made his way downstairs to the bar. The place was filled with hotel guests. One look at the crowded bar, and Steve knew there wasn't going to be any chance of chatting with Dillon. The bartender had his sleeves rolled up, and busily filled orders for two waitresses who were working the booths and tables. Steve pushed his way to the bar, and when he caught Dillon's eye he ordered a beer.

"Here you go, Doc," the crusty bartender said as he handed Steve his drink. "Went fishing today, did ya? Maude said you brought in a couple of trout. Not bad for a city fellow."

Steve couldn't believe the efficiency of the grapevine in this place. The way Dillon was smirking at him, he wondered if someone had seen the casting lesson Deanna had given him.

"My boy's the one who's going to be the fisherman," Steve answered with a friendly smile.

Dillon only grunted and busied himself with other customers. When Steve had finished his beer, he nodded at the bartender and said, "Well, see you around."

"I reckon," Dillon answered in a tone that made it seem there was some doubt about it.

Steve walked through the bar and went out on the terrace where he and Deanna had had their drinks the night Roger interrupted them. Several groups were enjoying the night air. Couples were standing at the railing or sitting around the terrace tables. Steve passed through the crowd and made his way down the stairs to the lower level.

This was the first time he'd had a chance to stroll the grounds at the back of the hotel. He identified the thick stand of trees where Benjamin Drake's body had been found. He looked up at the second-story windows and wondered what Penny had seen from her balcony that night.

As Steve stood in the shadow of the trees, he heard the sound of furtive footsteps and whispered voices. Pressing up against the trunk of a tree, he waited quietly until two figures broke free of the trees just a few yards from him. Then he smothered a chuckle as he identified Susan and Jeffery, the young desk clerk, holding hands as they disappeared through an unseen door in the lower regions of the hotel.

Young love, thought Steve with a wistful sigh. For five years, he had avoided any serious romantic entanglements and deftly sidestepped opportunities that came his way. His first priority as a single parent was raising

Travis. Although he enjoyed feminine company from time to time, he'd learned that most of the women he'd dated had one agenda—to marry a successful professional. He wondered if he was losing his perspective. He knew he was dangerously close to letting Deanna Drake affect him in a way that no other woman had since his wife's death. He recognized the deep feeling eating at him—loneliness. How did he know that his emotions weren't being carried away by the intensity of the present situation? She had aroused deep protective feelings, and a growing need to involve himself in her affairs was sending off warning flares. He definitely would put some distance between himself and the cloud of suspicion hovering over Deanna Drake.

He went to bed that night with this decision firmly in his mind, but his resolution came to naught.

The next morning it was discovered that the hotel offices had been broken into and ransacked.

Chapter Five

Deanna awoke the next morning to the jarring ring of her bedside telephone. With one eye squinting at the clock, she sleepily reached for the receiver. Five o'clock! Who in the world would be waking her up at that ungodly hour?

"Yes," she croaked.

"It's me—Bob. I think you'd better come down to the office right away."

"At five o'clock in the morning?" She didn't bother to keep the irritation out of her voice. His zealous dedication to hotel business was one thing, but cutting her out of a couple of hours' sleep was another. "What in the world is going on, Bob?"

"I came in early to do some book work, and found a mess."

"A mess? What kind of mess?" Her mind wasn't sufficiently in gear to even speculate what he was upset about.

"Someone got into the office. The place is a shambles. Drawers emptied, files dumped. Damn, the whole place looks like a hurricane whipped through it."

She sat up. "What? We've been robbed?"

"No. They didn't get into the safe. In fact, there's no

sign that they even tried. I can't figure it out. It doesn't look as if they were after money.''

She wasn't making sense out of what he was telling her. ''Not after money? What then?''

''Damned if I know.''

''Well, if they broke in—''

''They didn't break in. That's another thing that puzzles me. The outer-office door was unlocked when I got here, and I'm damn sure I locked it before I left last night. You're the only other one with a key.''

''I didn't go back to the office after dinner.''

''Then someone else must have a duplicate key. I've warned you about leaving your key ring lying right in sight on your desk. It only takes a minute to make a wax impression. Whoever it was simply unlocked the door, came in, wrecked the place and then left.''

Her stomach coiled into a familiar tight little knot. ''I'll be right down.''

A few minutes later, Deanna found the place just as Bob had described. The three small offices opened onto a front reception foyer, and the door leading to this area was the one that Bob had found unlocked. At the moment only two of the offices were being used by Deanna and Bob. She had taken the front office, Bob the middle one, and the office that Ben had used had been left vacant.

Bob was right. The place was a mess. File cabinets in all three offices had been emptied on the floor, and desk drawers ransacked. Deanna had left her late husband's office pretty much as it was after the police got through looking for possible clues as to who might have killed him. Someone had really given the room a going-over. Her eyes misted when she saw the picture of Penny that Ben always kept on his desk lying on the floor, glass broken and frame bent as if someone had stepped on it. This one vicious act alone sent a bone-deep chill through her.

None of it made sense. If this was the work of vandals, why limit their destruction to the three offices, when there were easier targets, inside and out of the hotel?

"We better call the sheriff," Bob said. "Maybe he can make some sense out of it."

Deanna nodded, but every cell in her body rebelled at the thought of having to endure Janson's presence and intrusion into her private life once again.

"We're in luck," Bob said after making a call to the sheriff's office in Silver Springs, the county seat. "Janson's on his way to Eagle Ridge on other business. They reached him by car phone and he'll be here in a few minutes."

When Janson arrived, Deanna held back and let Bob explain the situation. "Someone got in with a key, but it doesn't look as if robbery was the motive."

The sheriff examined the front of the safe and agreed with Bob. "Not robbery." After he inspected the three offices, he said, "The destruction looks methodical, as if they were searching for something." He turned sharp eyes on Deanna "Any ideas what they might have been looking for?"

"None," she said, meeting his prodding gaze without flinching. He wasn't going to put her on the rack over this.

"I reckon we won't know if anything's missing till you get this mess cleaned up. In the meantime, I'll talk to some people and see if anyone saw anything suspicious last night."

"We don't want guests to know anything about this,

Sheriff.'' Bob squared his shoulders as if he were back in the football lineup. ''You got it? We don't want any more bad publicity.''

''Then somebody had better keep his nose clean around here,'' Janson retorted. ''This smells like an inside job if I ever saw one. Someone had a key to the front office and waltzed in here as pretty as you please.''

There has to be a different explanation. Deanna desperately needed to keep the evil as far away from the hotel as possible. She couldn't have Penny exposed to another crisis.

''I'll set up some interviews for you with the staff, Sheriff,'' Bob said. ''But we'll have to swear them to secrecy.''

''Hmph.'' Janson snorted. ''You got about as much chance of keeping this thing quiet as a cat with its tail caught in a mousetrap.''

''We'll have to try,'' Deanna said.

Janson sent her an accusing look. ''You could save everybody a lot of time if you'd level with me for a change.''

''What do you mean 'for a change'?'' Deanna countered. ''I've been as honest with you as I know how.''

''I reckon that remains to be seen.'' He sauntered toward the door. ''I believe I'll have a little breakfast while I chew on this thing. Don't touch anything until I get a couple of my guys in here to get some fingerprints and see what else they can turn up.'' He turned and gave Deanna and Bob a long, searching look. ''You two are something else.'' He slapped his cowboy hat on the back of his head and sauntered out of the office.

''What in blazes does he mean by that?'' Bob fumed.

"Does he think we staged this fiasco to impress someone?"

"I don't know what he thinks," Deanna lied, knowing full well that Janson was convinced that she and Bob were somehow responsible.

STEVE KNEW something was wrong the minute he dropped Travis off at Deanna's apartment after breakfast. Susan said she hadn't seen Deanna that morning.

"She called me to get here an hour early." Susan's tone clearly stated that she wasn't happy about the change in time. "Some kind of emergency."

The young lady showed signs of a late night and Steve wondered how long she and Jeffery had dallied after he saw them. He decided to check on the new therapy room, just to make sure everything was in order for Penny's session that morning. It was a good thing he did. Everything had been moved, but very few of the items were in the same place as they had been before.

"Damn," he swore.

He put the mat down in the correct corner, and lined up the sandbox, toy shelves, painting easels and dollhouse along the same wall. There were some structural changes that he couldn't do anything about. The windows were facing the front instead of the side of the hotel. Maybe, just maybe, they had eliminated the disturbing factor that had governed Penny's behavior, and she wouldn't withdraw as she had done before.

When he was satisfied that the playroom was without any startling changes, he glanced at his watch and saw that it was only nine-thirty. He decided to let Deanna know that all was ready for Penny's session in the new room, and he made his way to the front office.

The lobby was almost empty, but that didn't surprise Steve. He had discovered that people vacationing in the mountains did not loll around half the day. An early riser himself, he'd seen fishermen around the lake almost before the rising sun sent slivers of pink light across the water. Jeep caravans were at the hotel early in the morning, picking up people for a day's outing to tour old ghost towns and mining camps.

As Steve approached the reception office, he saw Deanna coming out of the door with Bob. The hotel manager had his hand on her back. "It's going to be all right, Deanna," he was saying. "No harm done."

Deanna's smile was forced as she repeated, "Right. No harm done."

"Good morning," Steve said, feeling like an intruder but unwilling to walk on by them. He could tell from Deanna's expression that something more than routine business had brought her to the office at an early hour, and seeing Bob's arm around her brought lingering questions about the real relationship between them.

"Good morning, Steve." She moved away from Bob's hand, and her hostess smile was back in place. "I haven't checked on the new playroom yet."

"Everything's fine," he said, not admitting that he'd been working an hour to get the place ready. Deanna looked as if she had enough on her plate this morning. Maybe she needed someone to talk to—someone besides Bob Henderson. "I was heading for a cup of coffee. Will you join me?"

She hesitated and then nodded, "Yes, that sounds good."

"We've got to get to work on that IBM conference, you know," Bob said in a tone that could have been interpreted as a superior giving an order.

"Not today," Deanna said firmly. "If we get every-thing finalized by next week, that will be soon enough."

Bob opened his mouth as if to object, then closed it, turned on his heel and bustled away with the air of someone who had the responsibility of the whole hotel on his shoulders.

Deanna was silent as they walked down the hall to the dining room, and he remembered the way she had thrown back her head and laughed when they'd been at the lake. She was a different person when she was with the kids and away from the hotel. He promised himself that he was going to do his best to see that she had more time having fun.

When they entered the dining room, Deanna saw Sheriff Janson sitting near the back of the room at a large table with several of the hotel employees. Dillon sat next to Maude, and when the bartender saw Deanna enter with Steve, he leaned over and whispered some-thing to the cook.

Deanna stiffened and drew in a short breath. She should have known that the sheriff wouldn't waste any time talking to the staff. No telling what rumors would fly all over the place. There'd be no way to keep the break-in quiet now. She wanted to turn heel and walk out of the room, but she couldn't with Steve at her side. They sat down at a table out of hearing range of the large table, and as a young waitress brought them cof-fee, Deanna tried to compose herself.

Steve waited for her to say something that would help him understand what was going on, and explain why the sheriff was talking earnestly with a group of her employees. It wasn't in his nature or training to pry, but there were times when he wished he could jump into a situation with both feet, patience be hanged. He forced himself to lean back in his chair and make some benign remark about how good the coffee was.

She studied her cup for a long moment and then raised her clouded blue eyes to his. "I suppose you might as well hear about the break-in from me as from someone else."

"Break-in?"

"Well, not really. They walked in. Someone had a key. All of the inner offices were ransacked. Mine, Bob's and the one Ben had." She bit her lower lip. "Don't know what they were looking for. The safe hadn't been touched."

"Anything missing?"

"Not that we can tell so far. My files seem intact and so do Bob's. We can't really tell about Ben's, though. The sheriff had his deputy go through all Ben's stuff after he was killed and they didn't find anything suspicious."

"Do you think that now there might be something...suspicious?"

"No, of course not," she said quickly.

Almost too quickly, Steve thought. Was she trying to protect her late husband's reputation by her silence? Even as he silently asked the question, he caught her looking at him in a way that challenged his determination to remain detached. Her misty eyes and parted lips begged him to understand, and he knew he was dangerously close to promising his support no matter what the situation might be.

When the group sitting with the sheriff broke up, Janson came over to their table, pulled up a chair without an invitation and took out a pencil and his little notebook. "Well, let's see what we have here. Not much. Maude and Dillon say they closed up the kitchen and bar at the usual time. Didn't see anyone or anything out of the ordinary the whole evening. Young Jeffery had the night off, and went to bed early.

That's not true, Steve thought. *Jeffery probably didn't want anyone to know he and Susan had been cozying up somewhere in the hotel.*

"How about you, Dr. Sherman? Were you out and about last night?" the sheriff asked with his pencil poised.

"As a matter of fact, I took a late walk in the grounds before bed."

"See anything or anybody that might help us out?"

"I'm afraid I was lost in my own thoughts. I walked down to the lake and back and didn't see anything suspicious." *Just two young people hunting for a place to be together.*

The sheriff peered at him in a thoughtful fashion. "And you were alone? I mean, a good-looking fellow like you, and on vacation, and everything—" He let the suggestive sentence hang.

Steve laughed. "Thank you for the vote of confidence, Sheriff, but I assure you, I was quite alone."

"Hmm." Janson seemed to digest this like a cow chewing on cud, slowly and methodically. He peered at Steve and then at Deanna. "Neither of you saw Bob hanging around late last night, maybe keeping an eye on—things? He might have seen something that got his dander up, and..." He shrugged.

Heat flared in Deanna cheeks. How dare he imply that Bob might have ransacked the offices in a fit of jealousy? He was clearly suggesting that something romantic was going on between her and Steve, and Steve had lied about being alone. Even though it would have been a relief if the ransacking of the offices was nothing more than the result of Bob's misguided jealousy, she knew there was no basis for the sheriff's speculation.

"Do you have any other theories?" Steve asked in a way that closed up Bob's jealousy as an avenue of speculation.

Janson's sharp eyes settled on Steve as he side-stepped the question. "How's your work with the little girl going? Has Penny told you anything about the night her dad was shot?"

"Not a word," he answered honestly.

"You'll let me know if she does? Kids sees things. They'll talk about things that grown-ups try to hide." His manner made the statement more of a warning than anything else. "It seems to me you're in a position, Doc, to help unravel this knotty mess, if you've a mind to."

"I'll certainly try to do my best—for everyone," Steve said smoothly. He wanted to reach over and squeeze Deanna's hand for emphasis, but he knew how the gesture would be interpreted.

"Well, I reckon I'll be moseying on. Got to make a call on a rancher upriver. Somebody's been cutting heifers out of his herd. That's the kind of crime that makes wearing this badge worth the trouble," he said pointedly.

"I imagine some cases are more complicated than others," Steve responded.

The obvious sarcasm was not lost on Janson. He shoved his hat on his head and left with the warning that he'd be back to talk to Roger, Jeffery and some of the others.

Deanna managed a wan smile. "Sorry to put you through that inquisition. Janson obviously thought we were together last night."

Steve nodded and didn't pursue the subject. This wasn't the time to make it clear that being with her wasn't going to be governed by anything but her willingness to spend time with him. He glanced at his watch. "It's almost time for Penny's session. I guess I'd better get upstairs."

"How do you think she'll react to the change in rooms?"

"I don't know," he said honestly. He almost felt like crossing his fingers.

They might be back to square one.

Chapter Six

Hobo bounded into the new room without hesitation, but Penny's steps were slow and measured as she came in, looking around with guarded stiffness.

Steve sat in his usual place at the small round table, and acknowledged her presence with his easy smile. He didn't know what Deanna had said to Penny when she'd brought the little girl to a different location in the hotel, and he remained quiet as Penny's searching gaze circled the room.

Steve hoped that familiar playthings in their usual places would be reassuring enough to set her at ease, and he found himself tensing when she walked over to the double windows overlooking the front of the hotel. He waited to see if she would draw the blinds as she had done in the other room. After a moment, she turned around as if deciding what to do next.

Hobo was already sniffing around the table, and nudging Steve's hand for his daily cookie, but Steve pretended not to know what the dog wanted. He hid a secret smile when Penny walked over to the table, took a cookie off a paper plate and gave it to Hobo.

"Oh, Hobo wants a cookie," Steve said as if in surprise. Then he held out the plate of cookies to her. "And Penny?"

The little girl had always rejected the offer before. When she reached out and took one for herself, Steve mentally shouted, "Hallelujah." He knew that in that simple action was a validation of trust. In a rare moment of sharing, the three of them ate their cookies together.

Steve waited to see what Penny was going to do next. If she went over to the mat and spent the hour lying there in her usual listless fashion, he would know that she still didn't feel confident enough to venture out of her protective shell and let her four-year-old self enjoy all the things that were waiting for her.

As she wandered over to the toy shelves and stood there looking at them, he pretended interest in his notebook. It wasn't easy to remain silent and not offer anything in the way of a suggestion, but he knew that all initiative had to come from Penny. Superimposing any direction or authority could destroy the inner strength that he was trying to build up in her. He wanted her to feel perfectly at ease in this room, with no restraints, and the security to do what she wanted or just be herself.

Penny made another rather listless tour around the room, but instead of plopping down on the mat, she took a box of blocks off the shelf. Steve controlled a quickening of breath as she sat on the floor and began stacking several blocks one on top of the other.

Good, he thought. The activity was purposeful.

Very carefully Penny made a tower out of a half-dozen blocks. She looked at her creation for a long moment, and then she gave it a vicious slap of her hand and sent the blocks scattering across the floor.

She shot a quick look at him to see what he was

going to do or say. When he ignored her, she took more blocks out of the box. She built another tower, and another, each time knocking it over with an angry force until there were no blocks left in the box.

Her emotion spent, she sat on the floor looking desolate. Then she pulled her knees up, laid her head against them, and her little shoulders trembled as if with silent sobs.

Steve got up from his cushion and sat quietly down on the floor beside her, but did not touch her. He steeled himself against the temptation to pull her into his comforting arms and promise her that everything was going to be all right. Already the little girl had touched his heart in a personal way that made it difficult to hold back his own feelings. He knew he would do more harm than good if he allowed himself to cuddle her without her inviting the intimacy. His goal was to help Penny develop an emotional strength within herself that would allow her to face whatever demons had destroyed her sense of security. She had to come to terms with her own fears—and her own anger. Her fierce tumbling of the blocks was encouraging. Once the anger was released, other emotions could take its place, and whatever had made her retreat could be faced.

They sat quietly on the floor side by side until the timer rang. Penny raised her head, and Steve said, "Time to go."

As they got to their feet, he saw that her cheeks were tear-stained. Deanna had put Penny's blond hair in pigtails tied with pretty red bows, and some wayward curls had fallen down on her forehead. Her red-checkered sunsuit and white sandals made her look like a little girl ready for play, Steve thought, but her haunted eyes and the tears on her face belied the carefree life of a four-year-old.

Steve had started walking Penny back to the apartment after each session instead of making Deanna drop whatever she was doing to come and get her. He didn't know what Deanna would have to say about him bringing her daughter back looking worn-out and tearful. Some parents could not stand seeing their child put through an emotional ringer, session after session.

Steve's concerns about what Deanna would think faded instantly a moment later as his heart leaped with joy. He wanted to laugh aloud because Penny took his hand as they walked down the stairs together, Hobo trailing behind them. It was the first overture that the little girl had ever made toward him.

Susan took one look at Penny's tear-streaked face and gasped. She sent a demanding glare at Steve. "What happened to her?"

"She had a little cry," Steve said honestly in a matter-of-fact voice. "But she's fine now. Aren't you, Penny?" He gave the little hand a squeeze. "You can help her wash up for lunch, Susan. Where's Travis?"

She gave her head a jerk toward the balcony. "He's sitting out there watching the fishing boats. I think he's got it in his head you're going to rent one this afternoon," she warned him.

He didn't see Deanna as they had a quick lunch, and Susan said that she was busy overseeing activities for a Denver women's group who was having a conference at the hotel.

Steve decided that sitting idly in a boat would give him a chance to do some thinking, and much to Travis's delight they spent the afternoon fishing on the lake.

"Isn't this great, Dad? Can we build our own fire and

cook 'em?'' The fact that they got only a few bites and landed only two small fish didn't seem to stop Travis's enthusiasm.

"Sure, why not." There were outdoor grills scattered around the lake for hotel guests. Travis winced a little as they gutted the two fish, but when they were cooked, the boy ate his with true fisherman gusto. Steve's heart filled with tenderness for his son. It was hard being both father and mother, but the close bond between them was a blessing, and Steve was more convinced than ever that this move to Colorado had been a good one for both of them. He wanted more times together like this mountain vacation.

That evening, Steve recorded his notes on the laptop and reviewed the progress Penny had made that morning. Even though he'd successfully brought about positive changes in the personality and behavior of many disturbed children, what made this case different from all the rest—he was honest enough with himself to admit it—was personal involvement that went beyond just a patient-therapist relationship. The little girl had begun to weave strings around his heart. He had better watch himself or his emotional attachment could end up clouding his judgment.

They returned to the hotel late afternoon, showered and changed clothes. Travis wanted to stay in their room and watch television, so Steve wandered downstairs, hoping to have a word with Deanna about the morning's session. Here again, he was allowing his emotions to tread dangerous waters. No use trying to deny that he found Penny's mother extremely attractive, and looked forward to her company. He wanted to believe that she was an innocent victim in the tragic murder of her husband—but what if she wasn't? And what if his success with Penny proved that she had been lying to him, and everyone else? He shoved aside such negative thoughts. If he couldn't trust his judgment about people, he'd better get into a different profession.

He checked her office, the dining room and had just stepped into the lounge at happy hour when he heard someone call his name. A very attractive brunette in a revealing backless sundress smiled broadly and motioned him over to her nearby table. "Dr. Sherman. What a nice surprise to see you again." She held out her hand. "You may not remember me. Vanessa Brockman, president of St. Andrew's Hospital Auxiliary. You spoke at our May luncheon."

"Oh, yes, of course." Steve did remember her, expensive clothes, well-groomed, socialite manners and a little pushy in her own way.

"We enjoyed your talk so much."

"Thank you. A very nice group of ladies," he said gallantly. The invitation to speak to the group had come only a few weeks after he'd arrived in Denver, when the *Denver Post* had done a short story on him and his work with traumatized children.

"Our auxiliary is here on a weekend retreat," she told him. "I think you'll be pleased with our plans to build a spacious home for children undergoing psychiatric treatment. Please join me and I'll tell you about it."

Smart lady, Steve thought. She had worded the invitation in such a way that a refusal would be a rebuff to the project. No sign of a wedding ring, he noticed as he sat down. Ah yes, the mating game. He'd bet Vanessa Brockman was a rich divorcée deftly using charity works to keep her name in front of the public and eligible escorts at her elbow. He knew the type, but encouraging her to work for the Children's Trauma House was worth a few minutes of his time. He caught Dillon eyeing him and Vanessa. *Pickup time,* the bartender's knowing smirk seemed to say.

"What are you drinking?" Vanessa asked. She motioned for the cocktail waitress, and Steve ordered a scotch and soda.

"We'd be delighted if you wanted to join us for any of our sessions."

"Thank you, but my son and I are enjoying a few weeks of leisure time," he said with a firm smile. "Tell me about this new project of yours."

Obviously, Vanessa was more interested in talking about him than the project, and she quickly changed the subject. "How are you liking Colorado so far? You're not finding us too provincial, I hope," she said with a flirtatious laugh.

Steve silently groaned, but managed a polite, "Not at all. Travis and I are thoroughly enjoying ourselves."

"So your little boy is here with you," she said as if a child wasn't in her picture of the eligible doctor in need of company. "I guess there isn't all that much to do at Eagle Ridge. You really should visit some of the other resort areas." She launched into an enthusiastic recital of some of the offerings at the bigger hotels in Vail and Aspen.

"I suppose if you're into razzle-dazzle, they have more to offer." His tone indicated that wasn't his lifestyle. "I prefer a hotel like this one, which offers comfort and genuine beauty. I think your group was wise to select it for your conference."

Vanessa smiled, but he could tell that it hadn't been her idea to come to Eagle Ridge.

Steve didn't see Deanna when she glanced in the tavern a few minutes later, looking for him. Susan had told her that Penny had come back teary-eyed from her session, and Deanna had been anxious to talk with him. When she saw that he was having a drink with Vanessa Brockman, one of the women who was at the hotel for a hospital auxiliary's weekend retreat, she was tempted to intrude, but restrained the impulse. Obviously, he had other things on his mind at the moment. The fashionable Ms. Brockman was leaning toward him, smiling as she talked, and Dr. Sherman seemed fascinated by what she was saying.

Deanna turned away and headed for the kitchen. The day had been one from hell. She'd done her best to provide the kind of accommodations that Vanessa Brockman and her ladies wanted for their weekend retreat, but it was clear they would have been happier at one of the chic Aspen or Vail hotels. They didn't like the menu that Maude had planned for their luncheon, and when Deanna had asked her to change it, the cook had slammed around the kitchen, audibly swearing in her gruff voice. Hopefully Deanna could smooth things over with Maude before the day ended.

"How are things going with you and your nephew?" Deanna asked, trying to be friendly. She still had her fingers crossed that Maude wouldn't up and quit without notice.

"He's gone. Can't stay put, Roy can't. He's a drifter. When he runs out of money for drinking and poker, he moves on. I told him I wasn't givin' him any of my hard-earned cash."

Deanna couldn't help but feel relief. With Roy gone, Maude wasn't likely to up and quit. As best she could, Deanna smoothed over the change of menu with the crusty cook, then braced her shoulders and left the kitchen to deal with the next crisis.

Hosting Denver's elite women was proving to be a challenge all the way around. Deanna didn't know why they had chosen to come to Eagle Ridge for their conference, and in a way, she wished they hadn't even though she needed the business.

The sight of Steve and the stylish socialite was a barbed reminder that he moved in well-to-do social and professional circles. He probably dated a lot of women like Vanessa Brockman, educated and cultured, and one of these days he'd find someone who would measure up to the wife he'd lost. No doubt, he'd found a dinner date in the luscious brunette—and maybe more. The thought of them possibly spending the night together brought a spurt of undefined anger that she refused to recognize as jealousy.

Tired and weary, she chose to have dinner sent up to the apartment, and was relieved when Penny went to bed early. This was the first night that they hadn't eaten with Steve and Travis.

AFTER A LONG SOAK in her jet tub, she was still in her terry-cloth bathrobe when someone knocked on the door. She glanced at her watch. Only eight o'clock. It seemed much later. She shouldn't have been surprised to see Steve standing there, but she was.

"Oh, I guess you're not quite ready to go down for dinner," he said, eyeing her wet hair and the soft bathrobe. "I took Travis out for a hamburger and he's planted in front of the TV. When you weren't in the dining room, I decided you hadn't eaten yet."

"I had dinner sent up." She tightened the belt of her robe. "I was tired, and I thought you were probably dining with Ms. Brockman. I saw you in the lounge with her earlier.''

"Yes, she cornered me about a new project her group is sponsoring.'' Without an invitation, he moved past her into the living room. "I'm sorry I didn't check with you earlier.''

"I've already put Penny down for the night.'' As she closed the door and clutched the front of her robe tightly shut, she said, "I was just getting ready for bed.'' She nodded toward the bedroom that she and Penny shared. They'd moved into this apartment after Ben's death, and she'd planned to move into the other bedroom after a few weeks, but that had been months ago. She was still sleeping in one of the twin beds next to Penny's. "I've had a hell of a day with your lady friends.''

Steve noted the unmistakable emphasis on "your.''

"Oh?'' he responded as evenly as he could. "Did they give you a bad time?''

As she walked in the soft robe that hinted of nothing between it and her luscious skin, his senses were bombarded by her tantalizing femininity. In a sudden fantasy, he visualized the robe dropping to the floor and his hands tracing the lines and curves of her breasts, thighs and beautiful long legs. He forced himself to keep his eyes away from her supple body as she dropped into a chair and tried to keep the short robe snug around her.

He sat down on the couch opposite her and barely heard what she was saying about a to-do with the cook about a luncheon menu. "It'll be just my luck to lose Maude at the beginning of the season because of this weekend's hassles.'' She caught herself before she could dump any more hotel problems on him. "I'm glad you came by. I wanted to talk to you about Penny. Susan said Penny was listless when she came back from therapy, and she'd been crying.''

Maternal concern was evident in her voice and Steve hastened to explain what had happened, and assure her that Penny's reaction was a step forward. ''Penny has been holding back her emotions for far too long. The fury she showed in repeatedly knocking over the stack of blocks released some of the anger she's been holding inside. It's the first sign of any real emotion that I've seen in her. Maybe some of her defenses are coming down.''

He didn't tell her about Penny taking his hand for the first time. No telling when the situation might be right for her to do it again. One thing was certain, he didn't want Deanna pushing her to do anything that didn't come freely from the little girl.

''It's not fair that she should have to go through this,'' Deanna said in a strained voice.

And neither should you, Steve thought with a swell of male protectiveness. Never had he wanted to take a woman in his arms as much as he did at that moment. He cleared his throat, hoping that this rising desire wasn't evident in his voice. ''Penny is going to be fine. She's got a lot of inner strength—like her mother.''

''Thank you,'' she said softly. ''I needed that tonight.''

If she'd made even the slightest gesture toward him, all would have been lost. He would have pulled her to her feet and buried his lips in the moist softness of her breasts. His look must have betrayed the timbre of his thoughts, because he saw her eyes slightly widen in surprise, and her hand moved to tighten the belt of her robe.

He pulled himself together and got to his feet. ''I'm

sorry we didn't connect for dinner. I really look forward to the time we spend together, but I know you have your hands full with the hotel.'' He paused. ''Is there any chance we could make that hike up to Eagle Rock next weekend? It might do you good to get far enough away that people can't come running to you for help.''

''I'll see what I can do,'' Deanna promised, knowing he was referring to Bob's intrusion on the picnic.

She didn't walk with him to the door. Something held her back. Maybe it was the look of something akin to desire in his eyes, or maybe it was her own hunger that made her keep her distance. In any case she felt a strange mixture of relief and disappointment when he didn't linger.

Steve sensed her uncertainty. ''See you in the morning.'' He walked quickly away as she closed the door, and decided he was due for another shower before bed.

A cold one this time.

Chapter Seven

The next few therapy sessions brought a slow but marked change in Penny. Some of the toys, like the sandbox and drawing easel, which she had ignored before, became a daily choice of play. Steve couldn't have been happier with her choices because these were creative outlets, and they gave Penny a chance to express herself. Sometimes a faint smile would cross the little girl's lips when she filled a cupcake pan with sand and pretended to feed the cakes to the dollhouse family.

As he watched the child move more easily from activity to activity, he could tell that she was beginning to feel free enough to express herself in her fantasies even if the real world was still too threatening. He was relieved that she seemed to have accepted his presence in the playroom to be as safe as Hobo's.

He was especially interested in her paintings and drawings, and would study them carefully each day after he returned her to Susan. He took note of the progression of colors from the first dark smears to lighter shades. At first, Penny just covered the entire sheet of paper with scribbles, overlapping several colors and pressing so hard on the crayons that she sometimes broke them. When this happened she would flash an anxious look at Steve.

He'd smile and say matter-of-factly, "The crayon broke." Then he'd hand her another whole one from a new box.

During one session, Penny found a deck of Old Maid cards on the shelf and brought them over to the table where he always sat. It was the first time she'd made any effort to include him in her activities.

"Penny wants to play cards," he said evenly, trying not to show any surprise at this sudden willingness to interact with him.

She nodded and said her first word to him. "Deal."

He suppressed a chuckle, because of all the words he might have guessed would be the first one addressed to him, *deal* wasn't one of them.

"All right," he said and dealt out the cards. He pretended not to notice that she knew how to hold them and match up the pairs. He made sure that he ended up with the Old Maid, but she didn't seem to care as she gathered up the cards.

He had expected that one game would probably be enough and was surprised that instead of returning the cards to the box, her little hands began to shuffle them like a seasoned card player. As she deftly laced them together, a glimmer of a smile touched her bright eyes. She looked at him, put a finger up to her lips and whispered, "Shh."

He was so astonished that it took him a minute to hold a finger up to his own lips, and echo, "Shh."

She dealt out the cards with practiced ease, and this time he didn't have to pretend to let her win. She beat him, fair and square.

"Steve is the Old Maid again," he said, hoping for

more than a one-word exchange, but the timer rang and put an end to the card game and the surprising session.

Steve was anxious to talk with Deanna about Penny's first sound, as well as her aptitude for card shuffling, but he didn't get the chance. He'd only exchanged a few words with her in her office when they were interrupted.

Sheriff Janson stomped in, swearing and jabbing a stubby finger at Deanna. "Thought you could blindside me, didn't you? Looking all sweet and innocent. But I wasn't fooled, not by a long shot."

"What on earth are you talking about, Sheriff?" Deanna demanded impatiently.

"I'll tell you what I'm talking about. Gambling. Illegal gambling. Plenty of it right here under this roof. Thought you had everything covered up, didn't you? But you fouled up, lady. You fouled up good."

"Gambling?" she echoed. "But that's impossible."

Steve watched all the color drain from her face. Her eyes widened with fright, and she looked like a cornered animal about to be ripped apart.

"I'd take it slow if I were you, Sheriff," Steve warned as he moved quickly over to Deanna's side and put a hand on her shoulder as she sat behind her desk. "Throwing around a lot of accusations isn't the wisest thing to do. Why don't you just tell us what evidence you have for making these charges?"

"Evidence? Sure I'll tell you. There's a roomful of it in the basement room under the south wing. A nice little garden entrance for coming and going. All set up for some illegal poker and dice games."

Deanna looked blank. "What?"

"Don't play innocent with me, gal."

"I don't know what you're talking about." Deanna's

mind refused to take in anything he was saying. *Illegal gambling in the hotel?*

"You're the owner of this place. Are you trying to tell me you didn't know about the room?"

"Of course, I knew there was a storage room there. Ben told me that Dillon kept inventory for the bar in it."

"Hell, Dillon says he didn't even know about the room."

"And you believe Dillon?" Deanna's voice became strident.

"Any reason why I shouldn't?"

Of course he would believe Dillon. Good old boys always stuck together, didn't they? She swallowed back the bitter taste of bile, and her head reeled with a sudden roaring in her ears. Illegal gambling? Right here under her nose? No, it couldn't be. It wasn't possible, was it?

An unbidden "yes" stabbed her. A flood of memories swept back—Ben's late-night absences, his closed mouth about so many things and his determination to keep her from any involvement in certain aspects of the hotel business. He ran the hotel, and she helped out on occasion, but after Penny was born, her life centered around her child, not her husband or the hotel. She'd never argued with Ben, and their marriage hadn't been one of mutual sharing.

"Don't play me for a fool," Janson snapped. "You knew all the time what was going on, and for months you've been lying your pretty head off. You knew about the gambling."

"I swear I didn't."

Janson didn't even seem to hear her denial. "I wouldn't have found the room if it hadn't been for Susan and Jeffery. When I was questioning them about seeing anything the night of the break-in, they let it slip that they'd been cozying up in that room because it was the only place they could find some privacy.''

Steve decided that two could play a pointing-finger game. ''Didn't you search the whole premises after the shooting? Seems to me competent law enforcement would include a complete search of the place.''

Janson's ruddy face turned even more brick red. ''Ben's body wasn't found anywhere near that side of the hotel,'' he snapped. ''I didn't see any reason for my deputies to search the whole building and take inventory of the whole place. Now, I reckon I was the one that was too damn trusting.''

''What are you suggesting, Sheriff?'' Steve asked, wanting to take a poke at the man's accusing red face.

''That there was plenty going on when Ben took a bullet in the heart. And I'm damn sure his pretty wife has been lying to me all along.''

''I swear I didn't know.'' Deanna put fingers against her temples and pressed against a sudden stab of pain.

Janson snorted. ''You want me to believe that you never went in that room?''

''I had no reason to go down there,'' Deanna said as evenly as she could. ''Dillon was in charge of everything relating to the tavern, and I assumed he was using it for storage.''

Steve's quick mind examined this new development. ''Do you think gambling is connected to his murder in some way?''

''Does trash collect flies?'' he scoffed. ''Dammit, of course there could be a connection. Ben must have kept some kind of records about bets and money owed, but we didn't find anything when we went through his office right after he died.'' He eyed Deanna. ''Of course, someone could have gotten rid of them.''

''I never saw anything like that.'' Deanna quickly responded. ''I didn't snoop around his office, nor pry into his private affairs.''

Steve was pensive for a moment and then his eyebrows raised questioningly. ''Do you think someone else might have been looking for any gambling records? I mean, there seems to be no logical reason for the office break-in. Nothing was taken that can be identified. The safe wasn't touched. What if someone was worried about the illegal gambling coming to light and didn't want any evidence getting into your hands? The break-in would make sense, wouldn't it, if that were the case?''

Janson begrudgingly agreed. ''You might be right. If I had some names, I'd be on their scent like a bird dog.''

''And that clears Deanna, doesn't it? If she wanted to get rid of any evidence, she wouldn't have to stage a break-in to do it.''

Janson admitted, ''You should have been a lawyer instead of a headshrinker, Doc.''

Deanna sent Steve a grateful look. *He believes me.* Knowing that someone had put their trust in her made all the difference in the world. She looked Janson straight in the eye. ''I have nothing to hide. I'm glad this came to light. Maybe we'll get some answers now.''

He nodded. ''You can bet your boots I'll be talking to the staff again. Most of them weren't here four months ago when all of this hit the fan, but people talk. I might pick up a name or two.'' He stalked out without giving Deanna or Steve so much as a goodbye nod.

"Come on, let's get out of here." Steve took her hand and pulled her up from the chair.

"I can't. I—"

"Yes, you can," he insisted. "Susan's watching the kids. How about a little walk? Fresh air will clear your head."

"All right. I could use a clear head about now," she admitted.

As they left the hotel grounds and started up the side of a wooded foothill, Steve realized that Deanna's definition of a "walk" was really a "hike," or more precisely, a "climb." He was challenged to keep up when she left an indistinct path and climbed upward, making her way over several layers of sandstone rocks and jutting granite boulders.

"Are you part mountain goat?" he teased in protest.

Laughingly, Deanna threw a challenge over her shoulder, "Can't you keep up, city boy?" Fueled by churning emotions, she was grateful for physical activity that offered her some relief from taut nerves, but she knew she was setting a grueling pace for someone not accustomed to the high mountain air and rough terrain. She slowed down and allowed him to keep pace a few steps behind her.

Steve was totally aware of the strength and graceful movement of her lithe body as she moved ahead of him. The beauty of her sun-streaked hair and lightly tanned complexion blended in perfectly with the natural beauty of their surroundings, and the view of her rounded bottom and long legs molded by white summer slacks moving ahead of him was enough to fire any red-blooded man's hormones.

She glanced back at him from time to time, with an

encouraging smile. "The view's worth it," she promised.

He stared upward at the mountain of huge boulders that rose hundreds of feet above them. Surely she wasn't expecting him to climb to the top of that craggy precipice. "The view from where?"

She laughed and waved toward smooth sandstone rocks that made a natural sitting ledge on the side of the hill. "From here."

"Thank God," he breathed as he dropped down beside her on a wide flat stone.

Deanna noticed his breathing had quickened in the thin, high-altitude air and she felt a pang of guilt for setting such a demanding pace for someone used to living at sea level and walking along a beach. The fast climb had brought beads of moisture around the edges of his russet hair. As he sat beside her, she stilled an impulse to push wet strands back from his forehead.

"Whew," he grinned. "I didn't know that taking a walk in this part of the country meant scaling the side of a mountain."

She laughed. "Sorry. I'm so used to the climb, I never gave it a second thought. This is where I always come when I need to think about something."

Steve was pleased to see that the tight lines that had been on her face in the office were gone, and he could tell that the vigorous exercise had eased her tense muscles. She leaned back on her arms as the breeze off the lake below cooled the warmth of the summer sun upon their faces.

"There are eagle nests in these high rocks. If we're lucky, we may see one of the eagles sweep down and glide over the lake. Years ago, this whole area was a favorite breeding ground for them. That's how Eagle Ridge got its name.''

''It's a lovely spot.''

''What do you think of the view?'' she asked, motioning with her arm to high peaks cupping the mountain valley below.

''It's beautiful,'' he said, but he was more aware of her at that moment than the spectacular scenery. He'd been out with plenty of attractive women, and enjoyed superficial kinds of relationships that promised nothing but momentary pleasure, but as he sat there with her, he was aware of her every breath, and the brush of her body as she moved slightly beside him. When she turned and looked at him with her shining deep blue eyes, he knew that he'd never experienced anything like the swell of desire that overtook him at that moment. He instantly pulled back on the reins of his emotions.

With trained practice, he centered his mind on his professional responsibilities. He needed to talk with Deanna about what had happened during Penny's morning session. The incident with the Old Maid cards now took on another dimension. In light of the charges the sheriff was making about illegal gambling, he wondered if the little girl had been privy to some of these activities. Her ''shh'' indicated that she knew card playing was something to keep quiet about. He didn't want to bring up the incident without some kind of natural opening on Deanna's part. He waited for her to say something about the sheriff's charges of illegal gambling.

Deanna felt a change in his manner even though he continued to sit beside her and make comments about the spectacular panorama that surrounded them. She was perceptive enough to know that somehow he had removed himself from the closeness she'd felt when they first sat down. Clearly he'd withdrawn from any hint of intimacy. *And who could blame him?* What must he think of her? That scene with Janson was enough to put a bad taste in anyone's mouth.

The devastation of the sheriff's accusations came rushing back. Illegal gambling going on right under her nose? Even as she wanted to deny it, she knew it could be true. Ben had drawn firm lines about her responsibilities and his when it came to hotel matters. He'd also maintained his independent life-style after their marriage, going and coming as he pleased without confiding in her. She'd been surprised at his generosity with money, knowing that the hotel wasn't bringing in a large profit. Her stomach took a sickening plunge as she realized where the money must have come from.

Sick at heart, she turned to Steve and said defiantly, "I didn't know about the gambling. I didn't. I must have been stupid—stupid!"

"Not stupid," he answered quietly.

"What then?" Anger at herself made her voice ragged.

"Trusting, perhaps."

"Blind, trusting and stupid! I never questioned Ben about anything. I still can't believe I never had an inkling he was into gambling."

"Maybe there's another explanation for the room filled with gambling equipment," he offered, but without much conviction.

For a moment there was a quiver of hope in her devastation but it quickly died. "No. There were plenty of clues, but I ignored them."

"Did Ben spend a lot of time playing cards with Penny?"

She looked at him blankly. "Cards? With Penny?"

He nodded.

"I don't think so. Why do you ask?"

"I was wondering where she learned to shuffle and deal Old Maid cards so well. Have you played a lot of card games with her?"

"No. And I don't know what you're talking about. She's never showed any interest in playing cards with me."

She looked stupefied when he told her about Penny's willingness to play Old Maid with him, and the uncanny ability she showed in shuffling and dealing them.

"You didn't know she liked to play cards?"

"Maybe Susan's been playing with her and taught her how to handle the cards?" Deanna offered by way of explanation. "I don't think it could have been Ben, although he did spend a lot of time with her when I made frequent trips to Denver on hotel business." She frowned. "You don't think that he took Penny downstairs with him? And if he did, why wouldn't she say something about it? Before the tragedy, she chattered like a magpie."

He told Deanna about Penny's warning "shh." "This is wonderful progress. Not only did she volunteer a vocal response, but there was intention behind the sound. That's very, very encouraging," he said reassuringly.

Penny was beginning to communicate. Deanna's eyes were suddenly full, and for a moment it didn't matter what had caused her child to break out of her silent shell, but as her thoughts began to whirl, she looked at Steve in dismay. "Why would she say something like that?"

"She was probably told to keep quiet about the things she saw and did when she was with her father. Might have even been threatened, and this could be part of her traumatized unwillingness to speak."

"I can't believe my daughter knew more about what was going on in the hotel than I did. Why wasn't I sharp enough to sense that she was hiding something from me? I always thought we had a caring, loving relationship."

"None of this is a judgment on your parenting."

Deanna's belief that she knew everything there was to know about her daughter suddenly shattered into a thousand pieces. How many more things had taken place without her knowledge? What had gone on in her child's life that she didn't even know about?

"You've had a load dumped on you today," Steve said simply, with understanding.

She took a deep breath. "Maybe things will get better now? I mean, if Penny is beginning to open up, more things will come to light that will let us help her."

Steve nodded in agreement, but he knew from experience that the closer they came to understanding the little girl's trauma, the closer they might be to a memory that could bring danger upon her and the mother who loved her.

"We don't know what Penny saw from her balcony the night her father was killed," he cautioned. "She might have recognized someone, and the identity of that person is something her subconscious is guarding."

Deanna's shoulders slumped and a soft cry broke from her throat. When she leaned toward him, Steve's arms quickly went around her, pulling her close. She buried her head in the cleft of his shoulders, and he murmured reassurances as his hands caressed the soft sweep of her hair.

Deanna closed her eyes, comforted by the rhythmic rising and falling of his chest. Like a healing balm, his strolling touch soothed her jagged nerves. The warmth of his embrace eased the deep chill within her and when she lifted her face to his, her lips boldly sought the strong firm curve of his mouth. They melted together in a kiss that reached into the depths of feelings and desires.

When they pulled away, Deanna could tell from his expression that he had been guarding against something like this happening. They were both shaken by the intensity of the brief kiss.

She quietly apologized. "Sorry. Usually I can keep my feelings under better control than that."

"Me, too," Steve confessed, fighting a desire to forget about everything but taking her in his arms again.

Whoa, fella. Time to put on the brakes. This is no time to complicate an already complicated situation.

Chapter Eight

As they made their way back down the hill to the hotel, Deanna was strengthened by the comfortable companionship that had developed between them. She'd never needed a friend more in her whole life, and was grateful for his offer to do whatever he could to help her.

As they crossed the small clearing behind the hotel, they heard Travis yelling, "Dad. Dad. Up here."

Steve stopped, looking around, puzzled. "Where are you?"

"In the tree."

"What tree?" he yelled back. There were a dozen trees of various kinds in every direction.

Deanna pointed. "Over there. See them? They're up in Penny's tree house."

Looking higher than he had before, he caught sight of Travis and Penny in the midst of moving branches. The tree house was more a platform with a high railing than an enclosure. A ladder was nailed into the thick tree trunk.

Steve laughed and waved at them. "Tarzan and Jane, I believe. I hope Travis doesn't get it in his head to try and swing down from there. No telling what kind of games he'll think up. A tree house is a real treat for him.''

''Ben built it for Penny last year, but she hasn't played in it this summer. She's ignored the tree house since Ben's death. Even Susan hasn't been able to coax her into playing in it.''

''She seems to be enjoying herself now.''

''Yes.'' Deanna's spirits brightened. This tangible evidence that her daughter was coming out of her defensive withdrawal sent a quiver through her. What a blessing that Travis had come along with his exuberant energy and easygoing good nature. He was just the kind of playmate Penny needed.

''Come on up, Dad,'' Travis yelled, and waved.

''No, thanks,'' he called back. ''I've had enough climbing for one day.'' He pretended to move gingerly with exaggerated soreness.

''Flatlander,'' she chided, laughing. ''That was just a little hill.''

''Maybe, but my muscles are ready for a soak in the Jacuzzi. Will you join me?'' Steve was startled at how easily the invitation came to his lips. He knew better. What could be more tantalizing than that luscious body of hers in a bathing suit as they shared a warm cozy tub? Why was he so intent upon torturing himself?

Deanna searched his face for a long moment, and then she answered evenly, ''No, I don't think so. I really have to get back to the office. Bob will be on my neck as it is.''

Why don't you let him know who's the boss? As soon as the thought crossed his mind, Steve knew it was out of line. The business of the hotel should be none of his concern. His responsibility and obligation began and ended with Penny's welfare. She was his patient—not

Deanna. If he were completely honest with himself, he'd have to admit that his determination to be involved with Deanna was ninety percent male ego.

Deanna called up to the tree house, "Where's Susan?"

"With Jeffery," Travis answered. "She'll be back in a little bit."

Deanna muttered under her breath. She was paying the girl to baby-sit Penny, not to turn the job over to Travis and run off with her boyfriend.

"I think there's a hot and heavy romance going on there," Steve said, smiling.

"Not on my time," she answered curtly. "Sneaking around the hotel at night is something I won't put up with."

Steve couldn't help wondering if part of Deanna's displeasure was due to the fact that it was Susan and Jeffery who had brought the gambling room to light.

Before they reached the patio doors of Deanna's apartment, they met Susan coming out. "Oh, hi," she greeted them with a broad smile. "The kids are in the tree house."

"We know." Deanna's answer was as frosty as dripping ice.

Susan's round face fell at Deanna's tone. Steve watched as the young woman's defense system shot into action. "I thought it would be all right to leave the kids for a few minutes while I gave Jeffery a message," she said quickly. "They had a snack up there and I was just going to see if they wanted to take a swim this afternoon."

"That sounds like a good idea, Susan," Steve answered smoothly. Since he was paying her for the time she spent with Travis, he had the right to comment.

Obviously Deanna's anxiety over her daughter had made her fearful about leaving her alone for even a minute, and Steve didn't want an ugly scene to develop. "Deanna was saying that Penny hasn't played in the tree house for a long time until today."

"I know. I was really surprised when Travis talked her into climbing up there. It was all right, wasn't it?" She looked at Deanna for reassurance. "I made sure Penny got up there safely, and I told her not to come down until I got back. You never said you didn't want her to play there."

"It's fine for her to play there if she wants to," Deanna answered. It wasn't Penny playing in the tree that bothered her, but the fact that Susan had left the children alone while she ran off to give a message to her boyfriend. A deep-seated anxiety where the child was concerned created the need to know that Penny was never without adult supervision. *Maybe I'm too paranoid,* she thought. She decided to let the matter go for the moment. She'd already fought too many battles that day, and the inner composure she'd gained on the hike was fast disappearing.

"I think I'll join the kids in that swim," Steve said.

"Well, I've got to get back to the office," Deanna said briskly. "I've taken too much time off as it is."

"I guess that's a matter of opinion," Steve countered rather curtly.

The companionship they'd enjoyed on the hike was gone, and Deanna felt alone again as she turned away and headed for her office, praying that Janson wasn't there waiting for her with another bomb to drop.

IN HER NEXT FEW therapy sessions, Penny showed a slow but steady willingness to play with the toys in the therapy room. More and more she began to interact with Steve, and her one-word communications became commonplace.

When she'd hold up a doll from the dollhouse, she'd say, "Mother."

He'd nod. "Mother."

Sometimes she'd go through the whole miniature family as if introducing each of them to him—mother, father, girl, boy. She even included the toy cat and dog.

Steve always repeated the last object that she had named. As if Penny liked the naming game, she identified some of the toys lying on the shelves, and each time she'd look at Steve for approval. This verbal verification seemed to reassure her and it told Steve that she felt safe communicating this way.

When she found the clay, she brought her first creative effort for him to see. "Duck."

He was glad that she had identified the lumpy art object for him, because it could have passed for one of Dr. Seuss's imaginative creatures of unknown origin. He smiled and repeated, "Duck."

When her drawings began to take some shape and form, he was delighted. A rather disjointed figure of arms, legs, head and ears she identified as Hobo.

As if proud of her handiwork, she held the picture in front of the dog for him to see, but after a sniff or two, Hobo just wagged his tail and waited for something more interesting like cookies or a ball to come his way.

Sometimes Penny seemed bent on testing Steve's patience. Once she deliberately dumped a whole pail of sand on the floor, and then shot a quick glance at him, her blue eyes narrowing slightly as she waited for his reaction. When none came, she scooped up sand with both hands, and, walking all the way around the sand-box, she let it trickle on the floor.

"Penny is putting sand on the floor, isn't she?" He commented to Hobo, then went back to make notes in his small leather-covered notebook. Inside he was shouting, *Hurrah!* If Penny only knew how wonderful her belligerent behavior was in comparison to the leth-argy she had shown in the beginning. The little girl could put the whole room in shambles and it would be fine.

Although Steve was encouraged about the progress they were making, the days were flying by. Soon it would be time for him and Travis to return to Denver. Treating Penny in her home environment was certainly better than having Deanna make long trips to Denver, but there was no way of hurrying the little girl's emo-tional recovery.

Almost daily, Penny wanted to play a game of Old Maid, and Steve was more convinced than ever that the girl had spent a lot of time with someone, learning how to handle the cards. He knew if he questioned Penny outright, she would only retreat into her protective world of not talking. He had to wait until she was will-ing to open the door of communication.

So far, the little girl seemed unaware of the height-ened tension in the hotel. Susan had been sworn to si-lence around the children when it came to the interro-gations the sheriff was making.

The whole situation was an explosive one. Although Deanna tried desperately to keep rumors about the il-legal gambling from spreading to the community, Steve knew it would be a losing battle. Deanna would be smeared by innuendo, even if there was no proof that she had known about her husband's dealings. He wished there was some way he could protect her, but there seemed to be nothing but dead ends when it came to discovering who murdered her husband.

These thoughts were at the back of his mind when Penny sat on the floor with a drawing pad in her lap, scribbling away. She had quit making straight-line drawings and was now doing circles. In the beginning, all the circles had been overlapping, but in the last session, she had made a couple of separate circles into happy faces. When she finished a drawing, she'd sometimes bring it over to him with a look that expected his habitual comment, ''Very nice, Penny. Very nice.''

He glanced at his watch. Only ten minutes to go. He hoped she'd finish her drawing before the time was up, because she had shown resistance to leaving a toy or drawing if she wasn't finished.

He wasn't prepared for the sudden cry that came from deep in her throat as Penny grabbed the drawing pad with both hands and threw it across the room. Her wails were like those of a frightened baby as she covered her face with her hands.

''Penny, it's all right.'' He moved quickly to her side and sat down on the floor beside her. With a deep sob, she threw herself into his arms and buried her face against his chest.

''It's okay…okay,'' he soothed as he cradled her trembling little body. The timer bell went off, but they just sat there. Hobo came over and plopped down beside them.

Steve couldn't see the paper pad from where they sat, but whatever Penny had drawn had triggered a fierce emotional reaction. Maybe this was the breakthrough he'd been waiting for. A traumatic release was sometimes necessary before the child could return to normal patterns of behavior.

When she stopped crying and trembling, she became so still in his arms that he wondered if she'd fallen asleep. He held her quietly, until after a few minutes she raised her head and looked at him with deep trusting eyes as if he could make everything better. He knew that he had to say and do exactly the right thing to keep that trust, but before he could decide how to handle the situation, she spoke first.

"Bad man," she said clearly, putting two words together for the first time since she'd been his patient.

"Bad man," he repeated. "Penny drew a bad man?"

She looked at the pad and then back at Steve without saying anything.

"Can Steve see the bad man?" he asked, wondering what kind of a drawing could the child have made that frightened her so?

He was surprised when Penny willingly got to her feet, walked over to the pad, picked it up and brought it back to him. She stood there, waiting for his praise just as she always did when showing him a drawing.

The paper was filled with circles like so many of the last few drawings, but he saw with a start that she had turned one of the circles into a face. She'd put black dots for eyes, a blob for a nose and an ugly slash for a mouth, but what was more distinctive was a heavy black line like a mustache and jagged lines for black hair covering half the circle.

The skin on the back of his neck prickled. "Good job, Penny. Very good."

As she watched, he took the paper, tore it in several pieces and threw it in the wastepaper basket. "Bad man gone. All gone now."

She repeated in her frightened childish voice, "Bad man gone."

"Yes, all gone," he assured her, and wondered if she knew with the intuitive perception of children that he lied.

Chapter Nine

When Steve told Deanna about the drawing, she shook her head in disbelief. "I've never seen anyone around the hotel with a dark mustache and black hair hanging on his forehead."

"Obviously he was real to Penny."

"But why would she draw something that would be frightening to her?"

"I don't think she intended to. It's possible that Penny's been repressing the memory of a man's face, and the black crayon she had in her hand triggered it so she made the circle into a 'bad man.'"

This glimpse into her child's nightmare made Deanna sick to her stomach. Penny must have been filled with terror if she truly had been carrying that face of "bad man" around with her all this time. Maybe he was real, and maybe he wasn't, but Penny's fear would be the same in each case.

"Hey, it's going to be all right. Don't look so worried."

"I *am* worried. Don't you see what this means? Once the sheriff hears of this, he'll want to badger Penny with more questions."

"That's not going to happen," Steve said firmly. "I

won't allow him to question her. Absolutely no pressure can be put on the child or she'll retreat into her protective silence.''

She searched his face anxiously. ''Do you think she'll tell us what happened that night?''

''Sooner or later.'' *I hope sooner.* ''In the meantime, I think your idea of always having someone with her is a good one.''

Deanna paled. ''Do you think she might be in danger?''

Steve wanted to say no, but in all honesty he couldn't give her that kind of reassurance. ''Before the office ransacking, I wouldn't have seriously considered the possibility, but there are too many unanswered questions to take any chances.''

''Maybe we should wait and not tell the sheriff anything until we know more,'' Deanna said quickly as a quiver of fear began to curl in her chest.

''Is that what you want?'' Steve asked in a nonjudgmental tone. The decision was hers. No matter what the circumstances, he would never violate the confidentiality of patient and therapist, and as Penny's parent, Deanna had every right to keep silent about anything he told her. His professional responsibility was to enlighten her and no one else about the condition of her child. What she chose to do with the information he gave her was her business.

''I need to think about it,'' she said frankly, ''Maybe there isn't any connection between Penny's 'bad man,' and what happened the night of Ben's murder.''

''Maybe not,'' he agreed.

''And if there isn't,'' she said, thinking aloud, ''there's no need to send the sheriff bird-dogging in the wrong direction.''

"Right."

"But if Penny saw a dark-haired man with a mustache that night—" Her voice broke off and she looked at him with questioning eyes. "What do you think? Should I tell Janson?" she asked again.

"Do you think you should?"

"Blast it all," she stormed. "Can't you give a straight answer without patterning everything I say? Must you always be the cool professional?"

He felt like anything but a cool professional. He wanted to pull her into his arms and show her just how unprofessional he could be. Everything about her challenged a growing need to express the tenderness he felt for her. He wanted to cuddle her in his arms the way he had Penny, assuring her that everything was okay. He knew that she was being torn apart about the ugly accusations surrounding her and her late husband, and now she was faced with a decision that might affect the safety of her child. As much as he wanted to, he didn't have the right to influence that decision one way or the other. He was an outsider and he only knew what he had been told about the situation. What to tell the law officer and what information to hold back was something he wasn't in a position to decide.

"It's your decision," he said as kindly as he could, but she looked at him as if she was exasperated enough to slap his face.

"Thank you, Doctor," she said in a voice as sharp as a honed knife. "I'll let you know what I decide." With that, she turned heel and left him standing there.

ALL DAY LONG, Deanna vacillated between keeping silent and telling Janson about Penny's drawing. She was furious with Dr. Steve Sherman. One minute he acted like her friend, and the next, he threw up warning signals that she shouldn't depend upon him for anything but Penny's therapy. All right, if that's the way he wanted it, she'd be careful not to step across the line he'd drawn.

Deanna knew that her daughter's mental health depended upon encouraging the little girl to express whatever had traumatized her. Under normal circumstances, this wouldn't have been a problem, but there was the question of solving a crime. Deanna's joy that Penny had begun to express herself was coated in fear because of dangers the child's memory might trigger. The decision facing her mother was not an easy one. How much of what Penny revealed in the therapy room should she pass on to Janson?

Deanna still hadn't made up her mind when the sheriff came in the back door of the kitchen while she was talking to Maude about picking up some orders in the nearby town of Silver Springs.

"I can take my truck and run over to get them," Maude volunteered. "That is, if you want me to."

"Thanks. Let me talk to Roger first. I didn't know we were so low on supplies."

"Them fancy women cleaned us out last weekend. Never saw such a bitchy bunch."

Deanna smothered a smile. At least she and the cantankerous cook agreed on one thing. Deanna turned and greeted Janson, who had ambled over to a counter and helped himself to a blueberry tart.

Maude muttered audibly, "Moocher."

"Now, Maudie, don't get riled up."

"Don't you have something better to do than hang around my kitchen?" she snapped. "Seems to me you got a plateful right about now."

"You're right about that. Everyone around here must have been blind as a bat!" he scoffed.

"Gamblers have a way of covering their tracks," Maude muttered. "Roy would swear he'd never touch a deck of cards when he'd been up all night losing his shirt in a poker game."

"But how could heavy gambling go on right under everyone's nose?" Janson scoffed as he eyed Deanna.

"I can't tell if it's loyalty to you and Ben, or if there's been a meeting of the minds to keep their mouths shut. For crying out loud, I only want to do my job. I'm only trying to get the son of a gun that wasted Ben."

As they walked to her office, Deanna was still struggling with whether or not to tell him about Penny's drawing. She might never have told him if he hadn't started talking in a way that made her think he'd dropped his insistence that she must have known about the gambling.

"Yep, I've been thinking about Ben," he told her as they sat in her office. "Friendly enough for a good old boy. You know the kind, always ready to buy someone a beer and chew the fat. Ever since this gambling thing came to light, I can see how he might have been running the scam, all right."

He waited for her comment, but she only leaned back in her chair and let him say his piece. Everything he'd said matched up with the man she'd married and who had never really shared his life. Now she wondered how she'd been so blind.

"Yep, I reckon Ben was pretty darn careful about who got the word that there was action going on right under this here roof. If the game had been known locally, someone would have talked by now. My guess is that the players came from out of town and put up here at the hotel.''

By his tone, he made the last statement a question, but she didn't know how to answer it. Actually, she'd had very little to do with any of the guests after Penny was born. When Ben asked her to do some of the paperwork, she usually took it to the apartment so she could keep an eye on Penny at the same time. Sometimes they ate in the dining room, but not often, and she'd stayed out of the lounge because of Dillon's open hostility.

''I really don't know,'' she admitted. *There could have been a man with a dark mustache and black hair.*

The sheriff had been watching her with eagle eyes, and he asked with the swiftness of a raptor after prey, ''Did you think of someone?''

She knew that now was the time to tell him about Penny's ''bad man'' or keep quiet about it, and because the sheriff seemed more approachable at the moment than he'd ever been before, she was persuaded to tell him about the picture. ''There may have been a man who…who might have some connection to Ben's murder.''

''What?'' The chair that the sheriff had been tipping backward came forward with a thump. ''I knew it. You've been holding out on me. I felt it in my bones.''

''Well, your bones are wrong!'' she flared. ''I've been as honest with you as I know how, Sheriff.'' She took a deep breath to keep her temper under control. ''Something happened this morning with Penny that I think you should know about. It may be nothing,'' she cautioned. ''But I think you ought to have a look at this.''

Janson leaned forward with a look as greedy as a bird

eyeing a big fat worm. "What have you got? Did you find Ben's records?"

She shook her head as she took Penny's drawing out of her pocket. Steve had retrieved it from the wastepaper basket and taped it back together. She spread it out in front of Janson.

"What in the hell is this?" His eager expression was replaced by a furrowed frown as he looked at the scribbles and overlapping circles covering the paper.

"It's a drawing that Penny made for Dr. Sherman this morning. See this circle?" She pointed to the one that was different from the others because of its lines and slashes of black crayon. "This one has a face on it. See the black hair and mustache? Penny said it was a 'bad man.'"

He squinted at the paper filled with circles. "A bad man, is it?"

"That's what Penny told Dr. Sherman. She was quite upset by it."

"And all I have to do is show these scribbles around and I'll get a positive identification?" His tone was coated with sarcasm.

"Don't you see? This might trigger someone's memory. They might have seen someone who looks like that."

"Like this drawing?"

She nodded. "We thought you ought to know."

A flush of anger rose in Janson's neck and spread to his weathered cheeks. Anger like the red eyes of a bull flashed at her. "All right, you've had your little joke."

"Joke?" Deanna echoed, not believing that she heard him correctly.

"Hell, I know when someone's pulling my leg," he swore, jumping up with such force that he shoved his chair backward. He leaned over her desk. "You can tell your Dr. Sherman that I'm not the gullible old fool he thinks I am. If he's going to throw up a smoke screen, he'll have to do better than this."

She stared at him speechless as he grabbed the drawing, crumpled it and tossed it into the wastepaper basket. "I'm disappointed in you, Deanna. I had begun to think you might be leveling with me."

He stomped out before she could marshal her thoughts enough to defend herself. She sat there staring at the wall for a long time. Well, so much for the decision to tell him about Penny's bad man. Deanna sighed. She could have saved her breath. Janson's dismissal of the drawing put an end to any speculation that it might be important. *Or did it?*

WHEN DEANNA TOLD Steve what the sheriff's reaction had been, he was tempted to lambaste the old codger with scientific data about the workings of the subconscious mind, but he knew it wouldn't do any good. He just wished they had known what the sheriff's attitude was going to be before they shared the drawing with him.

"It's my fault," Steve told her. "I should have talked to him and laid the groundwork before we brought him into this. From now on, we'll be more careful."

A worried frown marred her pretty face. "What if the sheriff spreads the story around about Penny's drawing? Maybe he didn't put any faith in it, but somebody else might."

Steve had already been concerned about the same thing, but he tried to make light of it. "If Janson thinks he was the butt of a joke, I doubt that he'll admit it to anyone."

"I hope you're right, Steve."

But he wasn't. Both Bob and Susan came to Deanna and told her that the sheriff was in a tizzy because Dr. Sherman had tried to send him off on a wild-goose chase looking for a dark-haired man with a mustache just because Penny had made some scribbles on a paper.

"Is Penny beginning to remember what happened that night?" Bob asked Deanna. "That's the rumor that's going around."

Deanna wished with all her heart that she'd never mentioned the drawing to Janson. "We don't know whether the drawing means anything or not," she said honestly. "We told the sheriff because we thought it might be important, but obviously, he took the whole thing as some kind of sick joke."

"He's not real fond of the doctor, is he?" Bob asked in a tone that said the sentiment stated his feelings exactly. "It's kind of hard to put any stock in a guy who sits around playing with kids' toys."

"He doesn't sit around playing with toys." Deanna drew in a deep breath. She knew how Bob felt about the whole idea of Steve being there. Why bother trying to explain?

"You really like this guy, don't you?"

"If you're asking if I believe he can help Penny, the answer is yes." Deanna knew darn well that wasn't what Bob was asking, but it was none of his business how she felt about Steve. She vowed that from now on she'd think twice before adding to the hotel rumor mill where Penny and Steve were concerned.

As for Steve, he was less than pleased to hear that Penny's "bad man" drawing was the talk of the hotel and that the whole staff had had a good laugh over it. That evening when Steve went into the bar, Dillon couldn't resist taking a jab at him by remarking that sometimes the scribbles on his bar tabs looked like Popeye with dark hair and a black mustache. "You think I ought to see a shrink, Doc?"

"Might be a good idea," Steve responded solemnly. "Who knows, it might improve your sense of humor."

When Roger came into the bar, having finished putting the new part into the hotel van, he joined Dillon in making light of the drawing. "I guess I'd better be careful not to let my dark roots show," he quipped as he smoothed back his bleached ponytail.

"Ah, you're not man enough to grow a mustache," Dillon chided.

The only good thing about the whole fiasco, and the most important one as far as Steve was concerned was that Penny seemed more open and relaxed during her next session. There was no sign that the "bad man" incident lingered in her mind. If they'd opened a dark closet in her memory, the door had seemingly remained open and without any negative repercussions.

With less hesitation in her walk, she came into the room with Hobo bouncing at her heels. While the dog roamed the room in his usual fashion, sniffing at everything and munching a cookie from Steve, Penny ignored the drawing pad and sat down in front of the dollhouse.

Steve pretended to give all his attention to his notes, but as always he kept an eye on her. That morning she deliberately removed the doll family and all the furniture out of the house. When the house was stripped bare, and dolls and furniture were in a messy heap, she sat there staring at Steve, seemingly waiting for his reaction.

When he didn't pay her any attention, she said clearly with a flash of defiance. "Penny made a mess."

Steve started to repeat the sentence, but the words never got out.

At that moment disaster struck.

A piercing howl brought Steve to his feet. If Steve hadn't been concentrating so hard on Penny's behavior, he might have noticed the dog earlier. Hobo had plopped down on the mat, and now he was suddenly writhing as if in terrible pain.

Penny started screaming hysterically.

"What's the matter, boy?" Steve dropped onto the mat beside the slobbering dog. His mouth was open and his drool was brownish with a strong chocolate odor.

Candy. The dog had found some chocolate candy. Steve was baffled for a moment. A piece of chocolate candy shouldn't cause such a violent reaction. Unless? The truth stabbed him almost instantly. All the signs were there. Dear God! Steve knew with professional certainty what had happened.

Hobo had been poisoned!

Penny's wails were getting louder and louder. Steve turned and said in a firm voice, "Hobo's sick. We have to help him." He pushed Penny down on one of the floor cushions. "Stay there."

Steve always kept a medical kit in the therapy room in case of medical emergencies—and this was certainly an emergency. If he didn't get the poisoned candy out of the dog's stomach immediately, it would spread throughout his system and he could die a horrible death within an hour.

Penny's hysterical cries filled the room and Steve didn't want to think what a setback it would be to Penny's recovering if the dog died. He carried the writhing dog into the bathroom and spread papers on the floor. He would have given a hundred dollars for a stomach pump, but he'd have to depend upon a strong emetic to empty Hobo's stomach.

Penny disobeyed Steve's order to stay on the pillow cushion, and followed him as he carried the dog into the bathroom. Fortunately, he had a solution of peroxide in the medical kit. With Penny huddling in the doorway, sobbing the dog's name, Steve managed to get a fair amount down Hobo's throat. He didn't know how much candy the dog had eaten, but as Hobo began to retch up the sweets, Steve was encouraged to think they'd been in time to get most of it up.

As soon as he could, Steve grabbed the phone and called the front desk, deciding it would be quicker than calling Deanna's apartment or office. When Jeffery answered, Steve said curtly, "Find Deanna and tell her to come up to the therapy room immediately."

"Is something wrong?" Jeffery asked with undisguised curiosity.

Steve didn't bother to answer. His next immediate concern was Penny. It was important to give the child support without increasing her fears or lying to her. After Steve had carried the dog back to the mat, she had sat down beside Hobo. While Steve was on the phone, she stroked the dog's head in her usual fashion, sobbing.

He wanted to draw her into his arms, pet her and let her cry in his arms, but there was something about the way the little girl was handling herself that showed an independent spirit emerging. She had deliberately disobeyed his order to stay on the cushion, and even now she was looking at him through tear-filled eyes with a show of determination that surprised him. If any value could be drawn from this horror, it might be the materializing of her inner strength.

Steve eased down on the other side of the dog, and

was rewarded by a weak wag of Hobo's tail. *A good sign,* he thought, allowing himself a momentary sense of relief.

He said quietly to Penny, "Hobo's better now."

"Why he sick?" she asked with tear-filled eyes.

"Hobo had a tummyache. He ate too much candy," he told her, knowing that it wasn't just chocolate that had made Hobo so ill. *Candy. Where in blazes had the dog gotten the candy?* Even as the question stabbed at him, he knew the chilling answer. Someone had left poisoned candy in the playroom. And not for Hobo.

A moment later, Deanna hurried into the room. "What is it?"

The minute she had received the message to come immediately to the therapy room, her imagination had leaped full blown into all kinds of crises. "What's happened to Penny?"

"Nothing," he quickly reassured her.

Penny bounded to her feet and threw herself on her mother, sobbing. "Hobo...Hobo."

"It's the dog," Steve said quickly. "He ate something." He didn't want to go into the details in front of Penny. "I think he's going to be all right, but you should call a vet to look at him."

As Deanna cuddled Penny, she couldn't hide the relief that it was the dog and not her daughter who was ill. "Yes, of course. I'll call Dr. Timothy right away."

"I think it best if you take Penny downstairs now. This has been quite an ordeal for her."

"But I don't understand. Hobo was perfectly all right when I left the apartment after breakfast." Something in the set of his chin told her he was holding something back.

"We'll talk later."

Steve's tone sent a quiver of apprehension through her as she took Penny's hand and hurried her downstairs despite the little girl's protests of wanting to stay with Hobo.

"No, Penny. Hobo's going to stay with Dr. Steve for a little while," she soothed even as her own thoughts were churning with questions. *What happened? What is Steve holding back? Why was there a warning in his tone?*

She quickly found Dr. Timothy's number, called his office and asked if the vet could come over to the hotel as soon as possible.

DR. TIMOTHY WAS A SHORT, plump man with salt-and-pepper graying hair. After his examination, he nodded and said, "Poor fellow got ahold of something toxic, all right. Do you know what it was?"

"I'm not sure," Steve lied.

"Well, it's a good thing you emptied his stomach as quickly as you did. Hobo isn't going to be chasing any squirrels for a day or two, but he's a healthy dog and should be himself again 'fore long. I'll leave some medicine that should ease the stomach cramps."

"Thank you for coming so quickly," Deanna said.

"No problem. I had another call just down the road."

Steve didn't even want to think about how close they'd come to losing Hobo. *And what if Penny had found the chocolates first?*

As Dr. Timothy gathered up his medical kit, he looked around the playroom with frank curiosity. "I heard something about you working with Deanna's little girl."

"Steve is a children's psychologist," Deanna informed him. "He uses play therapy to help children like Penny."

The vet scratched his head. "Don't know how all this play stuff works, but I'm for anything that will help the little tyke. A damn shame Ben was taken out like that." He raised a bushy eyebrow. "I guess you're hoping she's going to shed some light on who did it."

"My main concern is Penny's well-being," he answered with a polite smile that put an end to the conversation.

WHEN DEANNA RETURNED after having put Penny down for a nap, she opened the door of the playroom and saw that Steve was standing with his back to her, staring out the front windows.

"Am I intruding?" she asked as she came in.

He swung around. "No, not at all. Just thinking."

"How's Hobo?"

"He's sleeping. Don't tell me dogs don't snore," he said in an attempt at lightness.

"The vet says he's going to be fine. Thanks to you." She moistened her suddenly dry lips. "Tell me what happened."

Before he said anything, he took her hand. It was cold and rigid in his grasp, and he knew that she had already prepared herself for what he was going to say.

He drew her over to the small table where three chocolate candies were lying on a sheet of paper. "I found these hidden around the room, and I don't know how many more Hobo scarfed down before he collapsed."

"Chocolates? That's what made him so sick? I know Penny has fed him candy before."

"It wasn't the candy." He said evenly, "Hobo was poisoned."

"Poisoned?" She echoed the word as if it lacked meaning. Then she stared at him as if he was going to say something else that would dissipate the ugly word that hung in the air like a vile thing.

"Yes, poisoned."

"That can't be."

"My guess is that the candy's doctored with something like strychnine."

"No, no." Every cell of her body protested the cruel truth of what he was saying.

He gently put his hands on her shoulders. "Deanna, we have to face the truth." Looking down into her stricken face, he said thickly, "I'm convinced that the candy was meant for Penny, not Hobo."

She closed her eyes against the horror of it. *Not Penny. Not Penny.*

He put his arms around her and drew her close. "I've gone over it in my mind in every direction that I can, and that's the only one thing that makes sense."

"But why?" She searched his face, knowing in her heart what he was going to say.

"It seems clear that even though the sheriff hasn't taken seriously Penny's 'bad man' with the dark hair and black mustache—someone else has."

Chapter Ten

Deanna struggled to deny what he was saying, grateful for the protective circle of his arms as she looked up at him. "Penny's drawing is responsible for someone trying to poison her?"

His voice was tense. "Nothing else makes sense. Her description might have hit too close to the truth, and the murderer could be desperate enough to stop her from talking any way he can."

"But how would he know about the drawing unless—"

"Unless somebody told him," Steve finished. He gently stroked her cheek with his fingertips. "We know that the sheriff was riled up because he thought he was the butt of a joke, and no telling how far the story got spread around."

"But whoever did this had to have access to this room. I mean, you lock it up before and after each session, don't you? And there's no sign of a break-in."

"Remember the office ransacking? They used a key to get in there. Who has hotel keys?"

"Just Bob and I." Even as she said his name, her breath caught for an instant. Could Bob be behind all of this? No, it was unthinkable. She had trusted him with too many things since she'd been alone. He'd never let her down, and he'd always shown deep concern for Penny. "There are only two sets of keys, mine and Bob's."

"Apparently, not any more."

"What are we going to do?" It was appalling that some evil person had total access to the entire hotel and could invade her privacy at any time. At that moment her whole world seemed to crumble under her feet, and she trembled with the horror of it all. She tightened her lips and blinked rapidly to hold back a sudden fullness in her eyes.

Steve knew better than to touch her again, but her haunted expression overrode his determination to keep a physical distance between them. He touched her shoulder with a reassuring squeeze, and as she looked up at him, he fought to control an explosive chemistry that fired every masculine cell in his body. He knew that he would have to use every ounce of willpower to keep his feelings for her under control, and the memory of how wonderfully exquisite she had felt in his arms challenged the strength of his determination. "It's going to be all right," he promised, speaking softly.

Deanna's heart quickened as the warmth of his touch on her shoulder sped through her, and she deliberately kept her gaze away from his face, knowing that her eyes and mouth would give away the desire she had to be in his arms again. And if he responded to her longing to be kissed, how could she ever be sure it wasn't just out of pity or sympathy? Her pride had already been shredded enough. She couldn't take any more rejection.

Moving away from him she fought to rein in her emotions. Bracing her shoulders, she said evenly, "We need to decide what to do."

As she avoided his eyes, Steve could tell that she was fighting against a repeat of what had happened between them before. He silently lashed out at himself for having touched her again, and created another tense moment between them. She had enough to worry about at the moment.

"What are we going to do?" she repeated.

He jerked his thoughts back to the crisis at hand. After a moment's hesitation, he said, "I don't think we have any choice. We have to tell the sheriff."

She grimaced.

"I know, but we've got the chocolates as evidence. Even a hardheaded skeptic like Janson will have to accept a lab report."

"I hope to heaven you're right," she snapped. "We've got to make sure something like this doesn't happen again. But how?"

His logical mind searched for some answers as he walked over to the window and looked down at the hotel grounds. A circle driveway was bordered by thick natural plantings, and some wide flagstone steps led up to the hotel entrance. Anyone had easy access to the hotel, day and night.

"We need to increase security," he said. "What if you let it be known that you're putting surveillance cameras throughout the hotel? I know it's an expense you don't need, but it could be a deterrent to someone furtively moving around the hotel."

"I never thought we needed that kind of big-city security, but when it comes to keeping Penny safe, expense is not a consideration. I'll make arrangements for a firm in Denver to take care of it."

"Another suggestion—the locks should be changed on your apartment and the therapy room. And all the windows securely closed from the inside. Someone will have to be with Penny twenty-four hours a day until this is over.''

''Will it ever be over? Will Penny and I ever have a normal life again?'' Deanna almost sobbed.

At the break in her voice, Steve said quickly, ''Don't think that way. The person responsible for all of this will be caught, you know. We're getting close and that's why he's fighting back. Would you like me to tell the sheriff about the poisoning?''

''Yes, please.'' Her lips tightened. ''Janson is set against believing anything I say. He's convinced I couldn't have been as blind and trusting as I was.'' She sighed. ''I have a hard time believing it myself. Anyway, you'd have a better chance of getting the truth through that hard head of his. I'll phone and ask him to come to the hotel.''

''No, I think it would be better if I went to his office. I want to handle this in a professional manner.'' He hoped that Janson would behave in the same way. ''Where is his office?''

''In Silver Springs, the county seat, not far from here, but it's about thirty miles over Rampart Pass.'' Deanna thought for a moment. ''Roger's going over there this afternoon for supplies. He finally got the van fixed. Would you want to ride over with him?''

''Sure, why not.''

''I don't know how to thank you for saving Hobo's life. I didn't know I was getting a vet and a psychologist all in one,'' she said with a weak smile. ''You'll have to submit a separate bill.''

''I will.'' He winked at her. ''And you may be surprised at the charges.''

His light, almost flirtatious manner did wonders for

her sagging morale. Once more she breathed a thankful prayer that she wasn't going through this horror by herself.

A FEW MILES OUT of Eagle Ridge, Steve wasn't sure he had made the right decision. Roger sent the van careening around mountain curves with the careless exuberance of a teenage driver. The view out Steve's window, a five-hundred-foot drop down a sheer mountainside, was not reassuring. He could easily imagine a car careering off the road and plunging downward to rest at the bottom of the ravine as a crumpled mass of metal. As Steve pressed his feet against the floorboard in a futile effort to help brake the car around hairpin curves, he shot a glance at Roger, who seemed totally relaxed in the driver's seat.

"Do you make this drive every day?" Steve asked him.

"Nope, just a couple times a week for supplies, unless Maude runs out of something. I wish it was more often. I'd rather be out on the road than hanging around the hotel. I'm not an indoor kind of guy."

"Deanna said you were quite a skier at one time. Too bad about your accident," Steve said, hoping the young man's bad luck didn't extend to road accidents.

"Yeah, a real bummer. So you're from California? I always thought I'd like to be one of those surfing guys. Maybe I'll head that way next year when I get a little money ahead."

"You might like it," Steve agreed. With his longish bleached hair and muscle T-shirts, Roger would fit right in with the beach crowd. Then he could easily trade his tag as ski bum for beach bum.

Even though the distance was only thirty miles between the hotel and Silver Springs, the road doubled back so much on itself that Steve decided it might as well have been fifty. The scenery was spectacular and Steve wanted to make the trip again when he could relax and enjoy the vaulting rock cliffs, green-carpeted mountains and the tiny silver ribbon of river wending its way along the canyon bottom.

Silver Springs was a booming little community with a five-block business district. Clusters of buildings included restaurants, bars, supermarkets, gas stations and some resort cabins and hotels. The streets were lined with cars, and there was the bustle of people along the sidewalks that gave the small mountain town the air of a metropolis. Roger pulled up in front of an ugly two-story brick building that housed government offices.

"The sheriff's office is on the second floor, and the jail is in the back," he said as if he might have been familiar with both. "Why don't I meet you later at the Rawhide Tavern when you're through. It's just a couple of blocks west on Main Street. I'll pick up the supplies and have a beer if I get there before you do."

"Fine." Steve had no idea how long he would be, but he hoped the sheriff would be in his office so he could lay out the situation in quick order.

A plain, unsmiling woman in her fifties sat behind a desk and gave him a curt nod toward the stairs when he said he wanted to see Sheriff Janson. He had a sneaking suspicion that she didn't know whether he was in or not—and it was clear that she didn't much care.

There were only three offices on the second floor and the door of the first was the only one open. As Steve glanced in, he saw Janson sitting at his desk eating a sandwich and reading the sports section of the *Rocky Mountain News*.

Steve gave a polite knock on the door frame. "Sheriff, can I talk to you for a few minutes?"

Janson lowered the paper, but didn't get up. "What's on your mind?"

Steve took the blunt question as an invitation to come in, but the sheriff's scowl didn't change as Steve sat down in a scarred wooden chair in front of the man's desk.

"I'm glad I caught you in," Steve said with easy politeness, but the remark did nothing to oil the wheels of hospitality as far as Steve could see.

"All right, Doc. I'm here. What's on your mind? This better be good," he warned as he reluctantly put down his newspaper and sandwich. "I'm in no mood for any more of your shenanigans."

"There's been an incident at the hotel that you need to investigate."

"I reckon I'll be the judge of that," the sheriff answered pugnaciously.

"This is something you can't ignore," Steve countered firmly. "Someone tried to poison Penny."

That caught his attention. Janson leaned forward in his squeaky chair and shook a warning stubby finger at Steve. "If this is another one of your 'let's tease the sheriff' jokes, I'll have your hide in a wringer."

"And if you don't act on this, I'll have your next election in a wringer," Steve answered in a deadly serious tone. "You can count on it."

For a long weighted moment, they stared at each other like two adversaries, then the sheriff growled, "All right, what proof do you have?"

Steve reached in his pocket and pulled out a small plastic container. "Here's your proof. Chocolates laced with some kind of poison. I found these scattered around the playroom. Fortunately, Penny's dog found some first, ate them, and nearly died.''

The sheriff eyed Steve skeptically, as always. "You're sure that's what made him sick?"

"Positive. Send the candy to a lab in Denver and check it out. Of course, I'm not a lawman like yourself.'' Steve failed to keep the sarcasm out of his tone. "But it seems to me that Penny's description of the 'bad man' hit home with someone, and it could be he wants to stop the little girl from doing any more talking."

Janson leaned back in his chair, obviously a bad taste in his mouth as he chewed on this new development. "How does Deanna fit into all of this?"

"Will you quit trying to make her the guilty party?" Steve snapped. "You can't think for a moment that she would try to poison her own child."

"I never said she was in this alone," Janson countered. "But this does put a different light on things. If the little girl's in danger, we'd best put our spurs to it.'' He frowned. "Are you sure that crazy picture of hers is all there is? She hasn't said anything more?''

At least they had his attention now, Steve thought with a sense of satisfaction, but he didn't know how much good that would do. Frankly, he had little confidence in the hometown lawman's sleuthing ability. No doubt most of Janson's law enforcement duties had to do with jailing drunks and running down speeding drivers. And yet there was a pugnaciousness about the man, Steve decided, that just might make him keep on the case like a dog worrying a bone.

When Steve told him about the precautions that they were going to take for Penny's safety, Janson nodded and even offered to have one of his deputies be visible now and again at the hotel as a kind of warning that the place was under surveillance.

Steve left the office with mixed feelings. He was glad that the sheriff was taking the matter seriously, but a sense of frustration remained.

Roger didn't show up at the Rawhide for nearly an hour after Steve got there, but was ready to down a couple of drinks before heading back. Steve firmly insisted that they leave after Roger had one beer. Maybe it was Steve's imagination but Roger seemed to drive the serpentine road with even more abandon. Steve felt like kissing the ground in gratefulness when they arrived safely back at the hotel about dusk.

Deanna had left the office for the day, and Steve found her and the children in the hotel playground. She had changed from her usual business wardrobe of trim slacks and shirtwaist blouses, and was wearing a pair of white shorts with a pink top that left little doubt about the beauty of her long legs and feminine shape. Steve's male appreciation took a jump just looking at her.

In addition to the traditional playground equipment, a rubber tire hung on a rope swinging out over a small pond that was Travis's favorite. He laughed merrily as Deanna pushed him out over the water.

"Hi, Dad," he squealed from the round circle of the tire as it turned and swayed from the long rope.

Other children, guests of the hotel, were playing on the regular swings and merry-go-round. Penny sat on a little rocking horse that moved back and forth with the push of her feet. She gave Steve a faint smile, and Hobo welcomed him with just a little less exuberance than usual.

"How you doing, boy?" He scratched Hobo behind the ears and the dog wagged his scrawny tail. That was the wonderful thing about animals, thought Steve. They didn't hold on to being sick, and seemed to forget once it was over.

Deanna gave Travis one last push and then walked over to Steve with an anxious smile. "How did it go? Did you get to see the sheriff?"

"I did. The meeting went well, I think," Steve reassured her. He was determined to be upbeat about the whole situation, but he mentally crossed his fingers that the sheriff really had paid attention to him. "Janson started out being his usual stubborn, opinionated self."

"That figures."

"But he listened to what I had to say. I could see his attitude change when I handed him the chocolates. With concrete evidence, he couldn't help but change his mind about a few things."

"I hope so," she said honestly. She was sick and tired of Janson and Dillon trying to tie her to Ben's murder. "It's time he put aside his prejudice and put some real effort into finding out the truth."

"I think Janson's come to the same conclusion. He's even offered to have one of his deputies visible around the hotel while he increases his investigation."

"None too soon," she answered shortly. She didn't share Steve's optimism that the sheriff would act any differently than he always had. Janson got elected every time because he was a good old boy who managed to keep on top of a few mini-crimes, but a full-blown murder investigation had pointed out his shortcomings, and she suspected that was one of the reasons he had it in for her.

"Hey, Dad, I'm hungry," Travis said as he bounded over to them. "Let's eat."

Steve laughed as he ruffled his hair. "You're always hungry."

"The dining room ought be open now," Deanna said. "I hope Roger brought back everything Maude wanted or there'll be hell to pay."

Steve could tell that she was dreading going back inside to face myriad problems that were probably waiting for her. "I have an idea. Why don't we all walk down to that hamburger place and fill up with junk food?"

Deanna hesitated, but Travis went into action. He ran over to Penny, "Come on, Penny, we're going for hamburgers and hot dogs. I'm going to have one of each, and french fries, too." He helped her off the rocking horse and hurried her over to where Steve and Deanna were standing. "We're ready."

"I guess I am, too," Deanna said with a laugh. "Travis, you're going to be the world's greatest success if you keep managing people the way you do now."

"I take after my daddy," he said proudly.

"Yes, I believe you do." She let a tender gaze touch Steve's face for a moment. "He has a way with people, too."

THE EVENING TURNED out to be one of those rare suspensions in time for both Deanna and Steve. Night breezes slipped down from high mountain peaks, cool and invigorating, and the four of them kept an energetic pace as they followed a well-worn path about a mile down the hill from where the hotel stood. They glimpsed scattered lights from summer homes on the hillsides, like misplaced stars against a forest-green background. Walking briskly, they passed cabins and campgrounds until they reached a small locally owned café. The smell of onions and charcoal-broiled meat greeted them even before they opened the door of Corky's Café. But the aroma wasn't in the least bit unpleasant. Inside, a holiday air filled the restaurant as vacationers laughed and satisfied their hunger after being outdoors all day.

Steve watched as Deanna visibly relaxed. *Good. She needs a break.* There were still slight shadows under her eyes, but she had apparently put the near tragedy of the morning aside for the time being. They exchanged grins when Penny happily wore a ketchup mustache after tackling her hot dog.

As they ate, Deanna intercepted some smiling glances in their direction, and knew that people thought they were a family. She wondered what it would have been like for her to have married Steve instead of Ben. For a moment, she let herself play on the fantasy, and her musing must have shown on her face because Steve leaned across the table and offered, "A nickel for your thoughts."

"Big spender," she teased. "I thought the going rate was a penny?"

"Not when your eyes glow like that."

She lowered them and quickly lied, "I was just thinking I'd love a hot fudge sundae with plenty of nuts and a cherry on top." It would never do to let him know how much she envied the wife he had loved so much. She deliberately kept the conversation impersonal, and was relieved when Steve followed her lead.

They walked back to the hotel in quiet contentment, and even Travis was quiet, listening to night sounds as soft as the rustle of needle-branches and bird-wings. When Penny got tired, Steve let her ride on his shoulders, and he was rewarded by a childish giggle and a whispered, "Nice horsey."

The evening was still young when they reached Deanna's apartment, but she hesitated to ask him to stay. Her momentary escape was over, and there was too much at stake to let her emotions get out of hand. She didn't trust herself not to invite an intimacy that they would both regret.

"I need to put Penny to bed. It's been quite a day," she said as he unlocked the door for her.

She could tell he was obviously surprised or amused by her polite dismissal, she couldn't tell which as he replied evenly, "Tomorrow then. I'll expect Penny at the same time." He lowered his voice. "Brace a chair against the door until you get the lock changed."

"The locksmith will be here first thing in the morning."

"Good."

"'Night, Penny," Travis said as she followed Hobo into the apartment. "See you later, alligator," he called after her, but the little girl didn't respond with the traditional reply.

Impulsively, Deanna leaned down and kissed Travis on top of the head. "After a while, crocodile."

Travis grinned at her and his twinkling brown eyes were so much like his father's that her chest tightened. After they'd left, she shut and locked the door. Then she leaned back against it, closing her eyes in a moment of flooding emotions she couldn't quite define.

Chapter Eleven

The next morning, Steve overheard a heated exchange between Deanna and Bob over the expense of the security systems. Anyone would have thought that the money came out of the hotel manager's pocket, Steve thought. Bob's proprietary manner about the hotel made it clear that he considered all major decisions his responsibility. It was obvious that in the five months since Ben's death, he had taken the hotel reins firmly in his hands, and Steve wondered how far he would go to keep them. Clearly, Deanna had her hands full trying to keep the reins in her own hands, and Steve felt easier when the locks on the playroom and Deanna's apartment had been changed, and the surveillance cameras had been put in place.

Penny's therapy was moving ahead, and Steve could see a marked change in the attitude of the little girl. She had begun to expand her interest in playing with the toys in the therapy room.

She'd lost interest in the Old Maid cards, and she seldom played in the sandbox anymore. The dollhouse still held her attention and every day she pulled everything out and then returned the furniture and dolls to the very same place. The only time she got mad at Hobo was when he poked his nose into the house and upset something. It was clear that Penny found security in having things in the dollhouse just the way she placed them.

She surprised him by beginning to use paints instead of crayons for her drawings, but so far her pictures were splashes of color, and nothing that resembled the drawing that had frightened her.

She surprised him one session when she picked up two play telephones and brought one over to the table for him.

"Penny wants to talk on the phone," he commented in a matter-of-fact tone, but he could scarcely keep his expression noncommittal as she sat down on a cushion beside him and put a receiver up to her ear, listening.

"Hello, Penny," he said into his play phone.

He waited, hoping that she would return his greeting, but she remained silent, and waited for him to say something else. His initial excitement that this might be the beginning of a two-way communication began to fade.

"I am talking to Penny on the telephone," he continued. "Is she listening to me?"

He was rewarded by a slight nod of her curly head.

"How are you, Penny? I am just fine. How is Hobo?" He smiled at her, and this time he waited expectantly for an answer.

After a long moment, he was rewarded by a whispered, "Fine."

"Hobo is fine," he repeated evenly, controlling the urge to shout in jubilation. "Penny is fine. Everyone is fine."

"Mama?" she asked in a stronger voice with her round eyes glued on Steve's face.

Trying not to look startled at this unexpected question, he answered, "Mama is fine, too."

"Papa gone?"

"Papa gone," he repeated. Had she connected her mother's distress with that of her papa's absence? Her next words verified the acuity of her little mind trying to piece everything together.

"Bad man gone?"

Steve's chest tightened. "Bad man gone."

Apparently satisfied, Penny hung up her phone. "Goodbye, Penny. Nice talking with you."

He was gratified when she continued to "play telephone." Even though the "game" started out as mostly one-way communication with Steve doing most of the talking, as the sessions went by, Penny began to contribute more. Her favorite subject was Travis, and when her sentences became more than one or two words, Steve found out a lot of things about his son that he didn't know before.

Travis hid from Susan.

Travis pushed someone into the pool.

Travis was going to swim across the lake.

Travis broke the candy machine.

As Steve listened to Penny's childish litany about his son, he began to wonder if the impression Travis was making on the little girl was altogether a good one.

Steve's notebook began to fill up with all the hopeful signs that Penny was coming out of her self-imposed isolation. He was certain that before long she would feel secure enough to begin talking about the night her father had been killed, but the expectation wasn't totally a happy one for Steve. The little girl's revelations might be a double-edged sword.

Deanna had already noticed a difference in Penny's

behavior. "She's talking a lot more now, has a lot more energy," she told Steve. "She's beginning to play with Hobo and Travis instead of just sitting and watching." Deanna's face glowed. "She's beginning to act like my own little girl, and I can't thank you enough. It's been wonderful to have you and Travis here."

"Just don't hold me accountable for all the bad habits she may have picked up from my son."

"Oh, you heard about the fracas Travis had yesterday with Maude?" Deanna was hoping that she could keep that little episode with the cook to herself.

"No, that's one I missed."

"Uh-oh, I guess I spoke out of turn. I mean, it wasn't anything. Just a boyish prank."

"And what boyish prank was that?"

Deanna gave a light laugh, trying not to convey the tension that had erupted when Travis got sideways with Maude. "It seems that Travis wandered into the kitchen just after Maude had set out a whole tray of freshly baked chocolate eclairs. Instead of taking one or two and scooting out of the kitchen before he got caught, he decided the safest thing to do would be to just take a small bite out of the bottom of each one. After all, such a small nibble wouldn't be noticed."

"So he ruined the whole batch?"

"I'm afraid so. Maude was about to clobber Travis with a rolling pin when I got there and rescued him. I've never known such a cantankerous old woman. If I wasn't desperate for a cook, I'd let her go in a minute."

"Travis never said a word about it."

"It's probably my fault," Deanna admitted. "I told him we'd forget the whole thing. He felt badly enough as it was."

Her voice took on a mothering tone. "Travis is a

wonderful little boy. So kind and generous. He's so full of life that he's bound to make mistakes sometimes.''

Steve couldn't hold back a smile because Deanna was using the same voice Travis's grandmother had used when she took over raising Travis after Carol died. Whenever the little boy got into trouble, she'd pleaded his case with Steve in the same way Deanna was doing now. As memories came flooding back, Steve realized how much Travis must have missed the mothering that his grandmother had given him when he was left without a mother of his own.

''All right, I won't say anything. Travis has an uneasy conscience, so I'll wait until he tells me.''

''Good,'' she said, obviously relieved.

This incident made Steve decide that it would be a good idea to spend even more time with his son, one-on-one. He was glad that Travis was happy being with Penny, Susan and the dog, but Steve knew that they would be returning to Denver in about ten days, and it would be a good idea to let Travis and Penny begin to spend time apart. Penny needed to settle into her own routine without Travis always being around. His concern was verified when he asked Travis if he wanted to go on a horseback ride that afternoon.

''Super keen!'' the boy answered with enthusiasm. ''I'll tell Penny.''

''No, Travis.'' Steve shook his head. ''This will be an outing for just you and me.''

''Not Penny?'' The boy thought for a moment and then nodded. ''I guess she's too small to ride a real horse.''

''Yes, I think so.''

Travis's expression brightened. ''Maybe they'll have a pony for her.''

''We can ask, and maybe take her with us next time, but not today,'' he said firmly.

''Maybe Dee can go with us next time, too.''

''Dee?''

''Penny's mother. She told me to call her that,'' Travis defended himself quickly. He'd been told that he wasn't supposed to call adults by their first names. ''She told me to,'' he insisted again.

''Well, if she said to call her that, then I guess it's all right,'' Steve assured him even as he asked himself if he had allowed his son to become too involved with Penny and her mother. *Just like you've become too involved?* an inner voice mocked him.

Steve's plan to spend time alone with his son was thwarted even before they left the riding stable. They were standing in a group lined up to receive their mounts, when someone touched his arm.

''Hello there. Fancy meeting you here.'' Vanessa Brockman smiled up at him under the brim of a white western hat.

Talk about a rhinestone cowgirl, thought Steve, the woman was decked out like a rodeo queen: red satin blouse, silver bolo tie and belt buckle and black western pants as tight as Saran Wrap. Her white leather boots alone must have cost her a fortune.

''Hello, Vanessa,'' he said awkwardly, totally surprised. He hadn't thought about the woman since that weekend she'd been at the hotel with her hospital auxiliary.

''I decided to come back to Eagle Ridge for a little vacation,'' Vanessa said in response to the questioning lines in his forehead. ''I just got in this morning, and at lunch I asked that nice Mrs. Drake if you were still here.'' Vanessa gave him a flirtatious smile. ''She told me you were going horseback riding this afternoon so I followed you.''

Thanks a bunch, Deanna.

Travis tugged at his hand. "Come on, Dad. It's our turn.''

Steve looked at the large horse tossing his head and tugging at the reins held by a ranch hand. He hoped the sudden dip his stomach took didn't show. "What about my son? He can't ride a big horse like that.''

The ranch hand pointed to a small speckled mare waiting behind Steve's big horse. "That's Dolly. She's nice and gentle. Don't worry. She'll give your boy a nice smooth ride. Would you prefer to have him ride in front of you?''

"Yes, I would.''

Without hesitation, Travis mounted the saddle with the attendant's help and eagerly took the reins.

With Vanessa and Travis both watching, there was nothing for Steve to do but climb onto his enormous old horse and pretend he was perfectly at ease as the clopping animal moved forward, following Travis's spotted pony.

The line of horses started up the mountain trail. Vanessa rode a palomino behind him, and Steve was certain she must be amused by the way he was bumping up and down in the saddle. Her mare seemed to want to hurry the pace, and kept its head close to the haunches of Steve's mount. He wondered if Vanessa was deliberately urging her horse forward in order to keep the distance between them short so she could keep up a commentary of oohs and aahs as the spectacular scenery unfolded in the valley below them.

For Steve, the only saving grace to the outing was that Travis was openly enjoying the ride. He kept turning around in the saddle and giving his dad the okay sign.

The ride was only about an hour, but it seemed an eternity to Steve before they finally reached a campsite that had been prepared for the riders.

Vanessa easily swung down from her horse and waited while Steve got off his mount in a less graceful manner. A ranch hand helped Travis down, and then their horses were led off to graze while the riders enjoyed their afternoon break.

Refreshments of sandwiches and doughnuts had been set out on picnic tables, and an old-fashioned chuck wagon offered soft drinks and coffee. A couple of guitar players went into action, strumming, singing and stomping their feet as they offered a selection of good old country music.

"I love riding," gushed Vanessa. "We had a riding academy where I went to college, and I even rode in competition a couple of years." She gave Travis a broad smile, and her voice changed to that pseudosweet that some people use with children and old people. "And I can tell this sweet little boy is going to be a real cowboy someday."

Travis's forehead creased in a boyish frown, and he looked at his father as if to say, *Where'd she come from?*

"Come on, Travis, let's get something to drink," Steve said, and eased past Vanessa as they headed for the chuck wagon. He was determined that the pushy socialite wasn't going to spoil this outing with his son.

Instead of sitting down at one of the picnic tables where it would be easy for her to join them, Steve took their drinks and picked up a couple of sandwiches off one of the refreshment trays. "Let's take a little walk, Travis, and find a nice spot to have our snack."

"Sure, Dad,"

There were a couple of worn paths weaving through trees away from the campsite, and one of them led to a grassy area where a mountain spring was falling through the rocks, making its way to the valley below.

Steve felt his spirits rising as he looked at the spectacular scenery. As he idly stared at the water spilling crystal droplets over polished stones, he decided that the view made the hour's ride on the rough horse worthwhile.

"Let's eat," he said as they sat down, cross-legged, on the grassy ground for their picnic. Steve was ready to enjoy the companionship of father and son, but they had only taken a couple of bites from their sandwiches when Vanessa showed up.

"Oh, what a lovely place you found," she greeted them merrily. "So much more pleasant than eating with the others."

Travis scowled at her, and Steve bit back a sharp retort. He'd never been good at handling pushy women, although he encountered enough of them in his profession. Because he was a young widower, more than one female colleague had considered him romantic prey, and intelligent women who should know better were always making excuses to confer with him on cases or attempting to include him in their social life. Vanessa wasn't the first influential society gal to intrude on his privacy in exchange for her support of a project of his. She could probably swing the house for disturbed children either way she chose. The stakes were too high for him to openly insult her.

"May I join you and this sweet little boy?" she asked with false politeness.

Travis glared at Steve, but there wasn't anything he could do but nod. *Talk about putting up with blackmail.* He sure wasn't in any position to fault Deanna for giving in to Dillon, and letting him keep his job so he wouldn't go to the tabloids with his sordid lies. There was a lot more at stake personally for her than for him. Just thinking about her made him realize how much he wished she was sitting here beside him. He remembered the companionable silence they'd enjoyed sitting on the warm rocks and breathing in the high, pine-scented air. The only silence in this situation was his and Travis's as Vanessa launched into a monologue about the summer she'd spent hiking in the Alps.

The outing was ruined as far as Steve was concerned, and he was ready to return to the campsite before the rest hour was up. When the time came to mount up again, even Steve was braced to endure the bumpy ride back to the stables.

On the way back, he was glad to see that Travis had recovered his good humor, and was thoroughly enjoying the ride on Dolly. No doubt his son would want to do this again, but Steve's backside was already protesting at just the idea of such a thing. Hanging his legs over a beast's backbone and getting battered black and blue was not his choice of a sport. He'd prefer a surfboard, water skis or a racket any day.

It was almost dusk when they finally returned to the hotel. Vanessa made a big production about seeing him at dinner, but Steve wasn't going to be trapped twice in one day.

"Thanks, Vanessa, but Travis and I are going to turn in early. We have a busy day planned for tomorrow.

Have a good time the rest of your vacation," he said with a finality that even she couldn't miss.

Steve decided to order room service for dinner as the safest way to elude the female predator. He was not surprised when his son's eyes began to droop heavily before the TV show was over that Travis wanted to see.

As Steve kissed him good-night, Travis looked up at him solemnly. "I don't like her."

Steve nodded. He didn't need to ask whom his son was talking about.

"She's not going to be my mother, is she?"

Steve gave a deep laugh. "Of course not. What gave you that idea?"

"Susan says you'll get married again."

"Well, believe it or not, Susan doesn't know everything."

"I'll have a new mother someday, won't I?" Travis wasn't going to let Steve drop the subject.

"Yes, if I marry again, you'll have a new mother."

"Do I get to choose?"

Steve sobered. "No, Travis, you don't get to choose."

"Why not?"

Steve sighed. How could he explain the intricacies of marriage to a sleepy little seven-year-old? "Remember the story of Cinderella and how she went to the ball and met the Prince? He fell in love with her and searched the whole kingdom to find her because she was the one for him. Well, I get to choose the right wife for me, but she'll be the right mother for you, too. Okay?"

"Okay," he agreed sleepily.

"I think I'll go downstairs for a little while." It was only nine o'clock, and Steve knew that once his son was asleep, he never stirred until morning.

The dining room was nearly empty, and the tavern crowd was thinning out because the band was just getting started on the terrace. Nearly all the outside tables were filled, and to Steve's surprise so was the small dance floor. Obviously a new bunch of guests had arrived at the hotel, and the atmosphere was one of laughter, drinking and dancing.

Steve looked around for Deanna and didn't see her for a couple of minutes, but when he finally did locate her, he did a double take. She was on the dance floor, and as a tall gentleman with slightly graying sideburns swept her around the floor, she was a Deanna Drake that Steve had never seen before. Waves of soft hair had drifted down on her forehead, her eyes glowed and her whole body radiated in abandoned joy. With each swinging step, her soft pink summer dress flared around her beautiful legs, and several couples moved aside to watch as she and her partner moved together to the rhythm of the music. The man was obviously a polished dancer, and Deanna followed his intricate steps with practiced ease. When the song ended, several people clapped, and Steve saw a flush rise in her cheeks.

Who was the fellow? A guest? Or her date? The man looked at least ten years older than she, but maybe she preferred older men. She'd married one, hadn't she?

Steve watched and waited, controlling the urge to walk up to them before the next song began. He saw her shake her head when the man held out a chair for her at one of the tables. Smiling, she turned away, and Steve moved forward quickly to intercept her, face-to-face.

"Oh, you're back," she said, smiling. "When you didn't show up for dinner, I thought you might have been...detained."

"No thanks to you. I owe you one for telling Vanessa Brockman where we were."

"Oh, was that a problem?" she asked with mock innocence. If the truth were known, she had given in to a spark of jealousy when Vanessa had asked her about Steve. *Maybe he'd invited her back to the hotel.*

"Do you like to see a man suffer?"

"Oh, I'm so sorry." A mischievous twinkle deepened the blue in her eyes. *He really didn't like the woman.*

Just then the band struck up a song familiar to Steve. Impulsively, he gave a mock bow. "Shall we? If you're not too tired from dancing with your other partner?"

"Oh, you saw? That's Charles Reney. He's got a franchise of a dozen dance studios across the country. Every year he spends a few days with us."

"Well, this will be a comedown, but I'll try." He slipped an arm around her waist and led her out on the dance floor. As they moved together, he knew he was stroking his macho ego, showing off, leading her in a dance that would have made Patrick Swayze of *Dirty Dancing* fame take notice. He made every step and every movement a sensuous expression of sexual desire as he pulled her to him, released her in a spin, only to be followed by steps that kept her one leg positioned between his. He smiled at her reaction as he let both of his hands rest on her waist, and moved her hips in a hypnotic sway that matched his seductive rhythm. He might not be as polished as her other partner, but dancing was a lover's art in California.

As the hot passion of the dance surged through them, Deanna knew that the harmonious movement of her body was communicating a dangerous message. All the latent desires that she'd held tightly under control threatened to break free as he moved against her, bending her backward in a sexy dip and arching his body over hers. She doubted that she was sophisticated enough to put aside the deep longing he had aroused in her once the music ended. Never before had she experienced the sensation of a man making love to her on the dance floor.

When the song ended, she withdrew abruptly from his arms. Certain that both of them would be embarrassed by what he would see in her eyes, she didn't trust herself to meet his gaze. "I really have to get back upstairs now."

She turned and walked stiffly away from him, and Steve knew that he'd totally mortified her. "I'll walk up with you," he said feebly as he caught up with her.

He didn't know what to say to ease the situation. At first, he'd really been showing off how well he could dance, and then things got out of hand. There was no use denying the sexual heat that had flared between them as they surrendered to the music and tantalizing steps. "You're a very good dancer," he said lamely.

"Thank you," she said stiffly.

Brrr. Icicles dripped from her voice. They reached her door in silence. When she took out her new key and inserted it in the lock, Steve was about to ask if he could come in for a few minutes because he didn't want to leave things so cool between them, but changed his mind when the door swung open and he could see into the living room.

Bob Henderson was sitting on the sofa. He put down the paper he was reading and stood up, waiting for Deanna to come in. As if Steve's surprised look had somehow put her on the defensive, she said, "Bob offered to baby-sit for me tonight while I made myself visible to our guests. Susan had a date with Jeffery, and I couldn't leave Penny alone.''

Deanna interpreted Steve's glare to mean he was questioning her denial of a romantic relationship between her and the hotel manager. Well, let him think what he would. She felt completely off base with him. Why had he taunted her on the dance floor that way? He must have known that her passions had been aroused by the seductive movements of his body against hers. A woman would have to be a stone statue not to respond, she thought with rising indignation. He should have had Vanessa as a partner. The provocative dance was just her style.

Deanna cleared her voice and used her business tone to say, ''Good night, Steve. I'd like to arrange a talk with you about plans to continue Penny's treatments when you leave. I know time is getting short.''

He nodded. ''Only about ten days left. I'll talk with you tomorrow.'' *So she trusts the guy with her daughter?*

He walked away before she'd quite closed the door, and he overheard Bob say something about the ''city doctor'' in a tone that didn't sound at all complimentary.

Steve's thoughts and lingering sensations of Deanna as they danced kept him from settling down when he got back to his room. He decided to catch up on Penny's records, but when he booted up his laptop computer, he discovered he'd left his small notebook in the therapy room. Hurrying upstairs to the third floor, he used his new key to get into the room.

He flipped on the light, walked over to the table where he always left the small leather notebook and stared at the empty table.

The book was gone.

When they finished the therapy session that morning, he remembered Penny had taken the sack of cookies for Hobo, and he'd neglected to take the notebook because his thoughts were racing ahead to the horseback-riding trip with Travis.

Had he misplaced it in the room somehow? No, he always made his record of the day's happenings sitting at the table. His notes contained everything that had transpired in the playroom. Someone would have a complete picture of the progress that Penny was making. He swore. Her steps toward open communication could be a threat to someone.

He stared at the shiny brass key in his hand and then looked back at the door with its new lock. *Who could have made a duplicate key in this short time?*

Chapter Twelve

Steve made a thorough search of the therapy room and his hotel room before he said anything to Deanna. When he couldn't find the small notebook anywhere, he stopped by her office the next morning before Penny's session.

"My daily record book is gone."

She looked puzzled. "That small brown notebook?"

"Yes, that's the one I use for taking daily notes during a session. Then I make a record of the notes into the computer each evening. Last night I went up to the therapy room to get my notes and the notebook wasn't there. I know I left it on the table after Penny's session yesterday."

"Well, I guess it's lucky you've got everything else on the computer except one day's notes. You can probably duplicate yesterday's session from memory, can't you?"

"Yes, of course. That's not my concern."

"Oh?" she said, still not grasping the gravity of the situation. "Well, if you misplaced it—"

"I didn't misplace it." His voice was a little tight, and he was reluctant to add more worries to the load she was already carrying, but she had to realize there was more at stake here than just some misplaced notebook. He was concerned that his professional notes in the wrong hands could put Penny in more jeopardy. "I'm sure that I haven't mislaid the notebook," he repeated more evenly.

She frowned. "Then what could have happened to it?"

"I can't be certain, but I've only been able to come up with one explanation."

"Oh?"

He could tell from her tone that she still hadn't tumbled to the reason for his worry over the loss of the book, and there was no way to sugarcoat his suspicions. "I believe that sometime between Penny's session yesterday morning and last night, the notebook was taken from the playroom."

For a moment she just stared at him, her eyes narrowing in thought. He could almost see comprehension begin to register, bringing with it all of the frightening complications that had struck him from the first moment he knew someone had stolen his daily records.

She moistened her dry lips. "But who? Why?"

He hated the way pain shot into her expressive blue eyes. He forced himself to keep his tone normal as he repeated, "Why would anyone want the notebook? I'm guessing that someone is interested in how much progress Penny is making. Everything that has transpired during my sessions with her is in that book. Penny's growing willingness to communicate is clear." He told her about the daily telephone game they'd been playing. "She's opening up more and more, introducing topics of her own. There may even be clues to what caused her trauma that aren't apparent to me but obvious to someone else."

The gravity of his expression created a familiar knotting in her stomach. She could tell that he was worried. "You mean someone deliberately stole it?"

"I don't see any other answer."

"Maybe one of the maids—"

"No one has been in to clean since yesterday's session. I know because I would have to let the maid in. The lock has been changed, remember? And we decided to have just two keys, yours and mine. I know that no one has had access to my key. What about yours?"

"I don't leave my key ring lying around. It's always in my purse, which I keep in a bedroom drawer, and when I leave the apartment, I take it with me. When I'm in the office, my purse is right here, in this bottom drawer. There's no way anyone could have gotten my keys without me knowing it."

"Then there must be another explanation." He waited for her answer. *Did someone else know where she kept her purse in the apartment or office?* "Any ideas?"

She shook her head. "What should we do?"

"First of all, we need to check the surveillance camera outside the therapy room."

Her eyes brightened. "Yes, of course. I'd forgotten for a moment that we had one. If anyone went in the room, we should have a record of it."

She got to her feet, and a few minutes later they had secured the film from the camera. Her heart was beating wildly when they viewed the film. *Who would it be?* Her nails bit into her hands as she clasped them tightly.

They saw the tape to the end, and the only persons coming in and out of the therapy room since Penny's session the day before were Steve and Penny. Whoever had gone into the room and taken the notebook had escaped the camera's detection.

"Whoever it is, is damn clever," Steve swore in frustration.

"I guess I'll have one more thing to tell the sheriff when he comes this afternoon," Deanna said in resignation. "Janson wants to meet with me about one o'clock."

"Did he say why?"

"No. When he called, his manner was brisk and official. I think we've finally got his attention. Either that, or Janson's found a new way to tie me to Ben's death, and he's ready to make an arrest."

Impulsively, he reached out and lightly stroked her cheek. "He knows your whole life is wound up in your little girl. He's probably got the results back on the poisoned candy, so he'll be looking elsewhere now."

"Sometimes I think I should just pack up our things and get as far away from this place as I can."

A haunted shadow came into her eyes and he wanted to tell her that running away wasn't the answer because evil had a way of following, but she needed his reassurance, not a lecture. "Dee, you're one of the bravest women I know. You'll see this through. I know you will."

"Thanks, Coach." She managed a forced smile. "I appreciate the pep talk, but I'm not sure I'm up to a heated session with Sheriff Janson. Would you care to join us for a one o'clock lunch?"

"Sure. He's one of my favorite people," he said with a sarcastic smile. "Let me tell him about the notebook."

"Maybe it will have shown up by then."

"Maybe." He knew then that she was still clinging to the idea that he had misplaced it.

PENNY'S SESSION went well, and Steve could see a marked improvement in her willingness to interact with him. Her new activity was tearing sheets of paper into small pieces and scribbling on them. When she brought one over to show him, she waited expectantly as if he was supposed to read what the scribbling said.

"Penny wrote something?"

She nodded. Her blue eyes had lost their guarded dullness, and there was a wonderful childish energy radiating from her. He wished he knew what game she was playing.

He squinted earnestly at the scribbles. "Penny wrote Steve a note." Then he handed the paper back to her, hoping she would give him a glimmer of what the scribbles said, but she just took it happily and went back to her pile of torn paper.

He knew in time she would tell him what the pretend letters said, but the special arrangement for these daily sessions was running out, and he'd only see her once or twice a week when he returned to Denver. Impatience almost made him gamble on pushing her in a way that could backfire and they'd lose the precious ground they'd made. He knew that Penny was beginning to include him in an inner reality that seemed safe. He couldn't destroy that by making any demands upon her.

When the session was over, she gathered up the scribbled pieces of papers and said very plainly, "I take to Travis."

Apart from the bad-man drawing, everything Penny had drawn, painted or made had stayed in the therapy room. This was important because it gave Steve a chance to examine her creations at a later time. He always gave her total privacy while she was in the room, never looking at anything she did unless she showed it to him.

"I take to Travis," she repeated, this time with a pugnacious set to her tiny mouth, as if she expected him to tell her she had to leave the papers in the room.

"You're going to read them to Travis," he said as a statement, not a question.

She nodded.

Good. That's better than me trying to figure out what the scribbles say.

Steve let the dog out an exit door at the end of the hall for his run, and then he and Penny walked a short distance down the hall to the apartment. He knocked on the door, pleased that Susan had followed instructions to keep it locked.

Travis had brought some of his video games, and he and Susan were just finishing a running battle to see who could build up the highest scores.

"Well, who's the victorious warrior today?" he asked, laughing at the loud groans and cheers coming from both of them.

"Need you ask?" Susan answered with a pretend frown. "Just look at his face. Pure gloating!"

Travis jumped up and clasped his hands over his head in a victorious fist. "The champion."

"I'll get you tomorrow," Susan threatened as she turned off the video and paused to give Penny a welcoming hug. "You two go wash up for lunch." Since the poisoning, Deanna had decided to keep a close watch on what the kids ate, and they'd started eating in the apartment instead of the dining room.

Not that Travis minded. His run-in with the cook over

the snatched eclairs had made him leery about anything Maude did or said. He still wasn't sure he was out of the woods with the tough old gal.

As the two youngsters bounded down the hall to the bathroom, Susan said, "I hope your son likes spaghetti and meatballs."

"Loves them."

"Good! Penny's appetite is getting better, but she still picks at her food." The phone rang, and Susan said, "Oh, that's Roger. He's checking to see if I can get off this afternoon and ride with him to Silver Springs."

Steve wouldn't have thought anything about it if there hadn't been a sudden visible flush on her face. As Susan picked up the mobile phone and took it in the other room for privacy, Steve wondered if the budding romance between her and Jeffery was on the skids.

When she came back, she gave Steve an apologetic look as she said, "Sorry about that."

"No problem." He decided a neutral subject was in order. "Silver Springs seems to be a nice little town. I rode over with Roger the other day."

Susan didn't follow through on his lead, but sat down on the edge of a chair opposite him and asked pointedly, "Dr. Sherman, do you think it's all right for a girl to change her mind about…things?"

"Well, change seems to be what life is all about." He wondered where she was going with this conversation and if he should stop it before it went too far.

"I've never been very popular with guys. Never could compete with those trim-figured gals." She shifted her rather ample buttocks in the chair. "This summer, I thought I was lucky to have Jeffery pay me some attention, but now…" She sighed. "Gosh, Roger keeps showing up. I know he's a lot older than I am, but he's so cool.''

''I see. And you're having some problem about dating him?''

''No. Yes. I don't know. What do you think I should do?''

''About what?''

''About dating Roger instead of Jeffery?''

''Is that what you want to do?''

''I don't know what I want to do,'' she retorted. ''Aren't you supposed to give people advice when they need it?''

''No, I'm not in the advice-giving business, but, maybe I can help you to decide what you want to do.''

Susan started to answer him, but whatever she was going to say was lost in the hubbub of two kids racing back into the room, ready for lunch.

Since Steve had promised to join Deanna and the sheriff later for lunch, he left Susan alone with the children. Since he paid her for watching Travis daily from nine o'clock in the morning until two o'clock in the afternoon, the lunch hour was included in her baby-sitting duties.

Deanna was already on the terrace outside the dining room, sitting with the sheriff, when Steve arrived. She'd chosen a secluded corner table bordered on three sides with a bank of greenery that offered some privacy.

''We were just about to order,'' she told Steve with a smile that left no doubt about the warmth in her welcome.

Steve couldn't tell from the sheriff's brisk nod of greeting whether or not he was displeased that Deanna had invited him. Not that it mattered one way or the other, Steve was more than ready to play tackle in Deanna's defense if necessary.

Janson seemed to be in a chatty mood, and not in any hurry to get around to the purpose for this little visit. He talked about the big Fourth of July Rodeo and Fair held in Silver Springs every year. "I've got a three-year-old quarter horse that I'm going to race. She'll kick dirt in their faces coming around the track. You ever seen a good old-fashioned rodeo, Doc?"

Steve admitted that he hadn't, and at the moment he couldn't think of anything that interested him less. Deanna was eating very little, and only managed a polite nod now and again. Steve's impatience grew when the sheriff launched into a long story of how Eagle Ridge's ranchers took about every prize at the races and rodeo.

"Doesn't training a horse to run take a lot of time, Sheriff?" Steve asked pointedly. "How can you fit it in with all your law enforcement responsibilities?"

Instant fury colored the sheriff's already ruddy cheeks. "I do my job."

Steve met his glare squarely. "We've been waiting to hear what the lab report was on the poisoned candy. It was poison, wasn't it?"

"I was getting around to that, Doctor. I came here to report to Deanna." *And not to you!* his snapping black eyes added.

Deanna leaned forward, thankful that Steve finally broke Janson's unbearable monologue. "What did you find out, Sheriff?"

Pointedly ignoring Steve, Janson answered her question as if Steve had never been in on the conversation. "Yep, it was poison all right. Strychnine."

Deanna shivered. "I can't believe someone would do that."

"I've been looking into the places in Silver Springs where they sell that stuff for rodent control. So far, I haven't come up with any Eagle Ridge names." He shot a cutting look at Steve. "Believe it or not, we country boys are not all green behind the ears. We've been turning over a few rows of our own. Just takes time, that's all."

"Maybe that's what we don't have—time," Steve countered. "Something else has happened."

The sheriff's bushy eyebrows went up. "What?"

Steve quickly told him about the missing notebook. "All my records about Penny are in it. If someone is worried about her progress, the evidence is there that she's beginning to communicate."

Deanna added quickly, "Steve is positive he left the notebook on the table in the therapy room after Penny's session yesterday morning. When he went to get it last night, it was gone."

"Didn't you have the lock changed on the damn door?" Janson swore impatiently.

"Yes. And only Deanna and I have the new key. What is more puzzling than anything is that the video camera doesn't show anyone else going in and out of the therapy room."

"Let me get this straight. The notebook disappeared from the room after you left it, but the camera doesn't show anyone going in and out of the door."

"That's right."

"And the only other entry is windows at the front of the building, three stories up."

Both Deanna and Steve nodded.

"What kind of a blasted game are you two playing?

'Trick the Dumb Sheriff,' is that it?" The ruddy color of Janson's complexion turned almost purple with rage. "Don't think you can muddy up the trail with some stupid 'closed room' puzzle." He shoved back from the table. "How do we know that you two didn't arrange that poison-candy ploy? And now you want me to go chasing after a missing notebook. Hell, all the smoke screens in the world aren't worth a cotton-pickin' damn when it comes to hiding the smell of a skunk. And there's stench in this hotel that reeks sky-high."

Before Janson could move away from the table, Steve stood up and faced him. He was outraged that the sheriff thought he and Deanna had dreamed up the poisoned candy and the missing notebook. "You can't believe Deanna would try to poison her own daughter."

"Penny wasn't poisoned. Just the dog. As for your missing notebook, I wouldn't bet a plug nickel that it isn't in your pocket this very minute, Doctor."

Steve clenched his fist. "And I'd bet you can't see your own feet for the blinders on your eyes."

"Oh, I see everything just fine." He slapped his hat on his head and added as more of a warning than a promise, "Nobody fools me for long." With a muttered oath, he headed down the terrace stairs and disappeared.

Deanna sat there stunned. She couldn't believe what had just happened. Like a vicious boomerang, everything they'd told the sheriff had come back to bury her even deeper in his suspicion.

Steve sat down beside her and took her hand. "Gosh, that went well, didn't it?"

Her chuckle was feeble. "Well, you can't say that Janson is inconsistent."

He agreed. "More's the pity. He's like a bull with his head lowered, plowing ahead, snorting all the way."

"It's amazing how well he can line up everything against me."

"I know, but I just feel that if he ever gets shifted onto the right track, we'll see some surprising results."

"Well, I hope it's soon, before—" she swallowed hard "—before anything else happens."

TWO DAYS AFTER his notebook had disappeared, Steve was still double-checking every possible place where it might be. "I know I didn't take it out of the playroom," he said aloud, mostly to himself as he and Travis relaxed in their room after a brisk hike halfway around the lake and back.

"What's the big deal, Dad? It's just a notebook." His tone dismissed his father's behavior as one of those stupid adult things.

"I don't like losing my records," Steve said flatly without elaborating.

"I thought you had everything in the computer?"

"I do. I just don't want that notebook to fall into the wrong hands. It wouldn't be good for Penny."

"Why not?" The little boy's interest suddenly quickened and he put down the comic book he was reading.

"Everything that Penny says or does in therapy is nobody's business. I'm worried about someone else knowing how much progress she's making."

"Why?"

"She might have seen something that would help us catch the person who shot her father. If we knew who took the book, we might have the answer to a lot of other questions."

Travis fell silent. Steve glanced at him, and then did a double take. He knew his son well enough to know that the boy was struggling with something.

"What is it, Travis?"

"Nothing."

As the minutes ticked by, Travis remained silent. He sat up on the bed, leaning against a pillow, not looking at his dad, and nervously fingered the same page in the comic book.

Steve waited, hoping his son would volunteer what thoughts were setting his mouth in a worried line, but when the minutes ticked by without Travis saying anything, Steve went over and sat down on the bed beside him. "What is it, son?"

Travis said anxiously. "What if nobody took the notebook?"

"Somebody took it," Steve said evenly. "We know that. It didn't just disappear into thin air."

"I mean, what if nobody bad took it?"

"That would be a relief," Steve answered evenly while his thoughts raced. *Had Travis stolen the notebook? But how? When? His son was never in the therapy room. And why would he want it?* "Do you know who took the notebook, Travis?"

Travis clamped his mouth shut.

"Travis, I have to know."

His son shook his head. "I'm no tattletale."

So it wasn't Travis. Then like a light coming on in a dark tunnel, Steve suddenly saw the whole incident in retrospect. At that instant, he felt like such a fool for not adding it all up before. With great effort he managed to keep his expression placid and his voice normal. "All right, son, I respect your loyalty, and I won't ask you to name the person who took it."

Travis visibly wilted with relief.

"But there is one question you have to answer, for Penny's safety, okay?"

The boy nodded.

"Where is the notebook now?"

With childish relief, Travis whispered, "In the tree house."

Chapter Thirteen

The tree house.

All the pieces of the mystery fell into place with beautiful clarity. Steve wanted to laugh aloud with relief.

Penny had taken the notebook.

She'd swiped it right from under his nose. Now he remembered the sack of cookies she had in her hands that day as they left the playroom. She must have put his notebook in the bag when she collected the cookies for Hobo. Steve didn't know why she'd taken it, but this was an insight that made all his anxiety worthwhile.

Steve bent over and kissed his son on the forehead. "You did the right thing, son, telling me. Why don't we pay a quick visit to the tree house."

"Penny won't like it."

"It's important, Travis. Important to her, and to all of us. We can't let that notebook fall into the wrong hands. Understand? Trust me on this. Okay?"

"Okay," Travis muttered, but he was less than enthusiastic about showing Steve the way up the ladder to the private little tree house that had become his and Penny's hideaway.

"Very nice." Steve nodded his approval as he bent

over to escape some leafy branches hanging over a two-foot railing that bordered the sturdy, well-made platform.

Steve followed Travis's lead and sat down on an old army blanket that served as a rug. The furnishings were simple: an apple crate was filled with toys, books and a couple of shoe boxes. A box of crackers and a can of peanuts seemed to be the extent of their pantry.

Steve didn't see any sign of his notebook, but held back questioning Travis about it. He could see that his son was fighting a sense of guilt for bringing his dad to Penny's and his private clubhouse. Travis was scowling as he sat beside Steve on the blanket.

"Dee was telling me that Penny had quit playing in the tree house until you came," Steve said with an approving smile. "You're very good for her."

"She's my friend," Travis answered, and then added in an accusing tone, "She trusts me."

"I know she does. You only want the best for her, don't you?"

He nodded. While they'd been at the hotel, Steve had initiated some open-ended discussions about Penny, hoping his son might have some insights that children often have with one another, but Travis had never shared anything that might help him understand Penny's emotional withdrawal. For the first time, Steve asked his son a direct question about her. "Has Penny said anything to you about the night her father was killed?"

"Nope. She doesn't talk much, you know that," he said in a grown-up patient tone that amused Steve.

"You'd tell me if she had, wouldn't you, son? It might be very important."

"She's never told me nothing."

"Anything," Steve automatically corrected.

Travis's eyes searched his father's face. "Dad, why does someone want to hurt her? She never did noth— anything—to anybody."

"I don't know why for sure," he answered honestly. "But I'm guessing she may know something about her father's death. That's why it's important that nobody else reads my notes about her. I have to have my notebook back."

"Are you mad at her for swiping it?"

"No, I'm not mad, but I've been worried. You see, I like Penny very much, and I want to keep her safe, just like you do." Steve watched his son's face, and waited. He didn't want to order Travis to hand over the notebook. They'd always had a close father-son relationship based on respect and honesty.

"Well, okay," Travis finally answered, and Steve silently let out the breath he'd been holding when his son got up, went over to the apple crate and brought back one of the shoe boxes.

"That's Penny's," Travis said. "She keeps her writings in it."

"Thank you, son. You're doing the right thing," Steve assured him. The shoe box was light, and Steve saw why. It was stuffed with pieces of papers like the little girl had taken from the playroom, and all of them were covered with illegible scribbles and happy faces.

"Did Penny read you her notes?"

"Naw. She just pretends to write." Travis scoffed like a seven-year-old. "She doesn't know her letters or anything."

At first, Steve thought his notebook wasn't in the box, but he found it buried in the litter of torn papers. When he opened it, he saw that Penny had added her own scribbles and drawings to almost every page. He smiled at this evidence that Penny had been aware of his note-taking every day, and had duplicated it with some entries of her own.

"She's a very bright little girl," he told Travis, smiling. He was about to close the lid and hand the box back to Travis when he glimpsed something else in the box. A small black book in the bottom of the box caught his attention because of the gold initials, B.D., embossed on its cover.

B.D.? *Benjamin Drake?*

Steve's heartbeat suddenly skipped a couple of beats. Had Penny's father given her an old record book to scribble in? *Or had the little girl made off with one of her father's notebooks, the way she'd made off with Steve's?*

As he examined the book, he saw that Penny had scribbled on every page, almost obliterating all the dates, names and numbers written there.

Steve didn't know what he held in his hand, but maybe, just maybe, someone had been looking for this book, the same way he'd been looking for his.

STEVE LEFT Travis on the playground with Penny and Susan, and went looking for Deanna. She wasn't in her office.

"I think she's in the kitchen with Maude," Jeffery told him as he shoved dark-rimmed glasses back on his thin nose. Then he lowered his voice. "Some kind of crisis over supplies that Roger failed to get. Maude's ready to wring his neck."

The sense of satisfaction in Jeffery's tone was obvious to Steve. So the young man knew about Susan's recent interest in Roger. Too bad, thought Steve. Jeffery seemed like a nice fellow, but definitely not a match for

Roger's extroverted personality. A young girl like Susan would have a hard time turning away the attention of a fellow who'd been around like Roger. Steve sighed as he made his way through the hotel. Maybe he should arrange to have another chat with the young girl.

When he poked his head into the kitchen, he was relieved to see that Deanna was just leaving. A background noise of Maude slamming around pans, and one look at Deanna's exasperated expression, told him that he'd missed the main event.

"That woman!" Deanna growled, clenching her fists. "For two cents, I'd fire her and do the cooking myself. She's the most belligerent, infuriating, demanding—"

"Whoa!" he said, taking her arm. "What you need is a good walk to get rid of some of that steam. Come on, let's take a hike around the lake."

"I can't. I've got to make a trip into Silver Springs. We've got a breakfast scheduled for twenty-five people in the morning, and I just got a call from Roger. The van broke down in Silver Springs and he's not sure when they can get it repaired. So much for his expertise as a mechanic. I should have told him to take the van in for repairs instead of trusting his mechanical ability. If I leave now, I can just about make it to Silver Springs before the markets close."

"Do you mind if I come along with you?" Not only did Steve like the idea of spending time with her, but the trip would provide a good opportunity to tell her about the notebooks.

"I can't promise that I'll be good company."

"I'll take my chances."

She gave him a swift smile. "All right. We'll have Susan watch the kids."

They took her car. He offered to drive, but she just

gave him a patient smile and said, "I think it might be faster if I drove. I know the road."

Nicely put, he thought, admiring her tactfulness, no aspersions on his driving ability, just an unspoken acknowledgment that she was probably the better mountain driver. He wasn't going to argue. In truth, he'd only offered out of masculine politeness and was relieved she'd refused the offer.

Steve had decided not to tell her about Penny's cache until they were almost to Silver Springs because he didn't want her thinking about anything but driving. He still remembered the way the narrow road skirted the edge of tremendous cliffs and precipices, and how easily a car could take a curve too wide and end up a crumpled heap hundreds of feet below.

He steeled himself for another tense ride, but after a few miles he realized that the trip to Silver Springs wasn't going to be anything like the one he'd made with Roger. He gave Deanna a grateful smile.

Late-afternoon shadows were already sweeping through an infinity of evergreen and aspen trees, and the canyons below caught the last rays of sun as the road climbed upward to a twelve-thousand-foot summit.

She eased the car around serpentine curves without coming close to the narrow shoulder as she drove the mountain pass, and he appreciated her smooth steady confidence. Her hands were firm on the steering wheel but not tense. He could tell that driving was helping her to relax and let go of built-up stress. Good therapy, he thought.

As if he'd spoken the thought aloud, she said, "I love to drive."

"I can tell."

Her graceful body molded the curves of the bucket

seat with tantalizing softness that made it difficult for him to give his attention to the view out the window. A redolent scent like a herbal shampoo touched his nostrils and brought a sensuous vision of her standing nude in the shower washing her hair. Even as he tried to push the erotic vision out of his mind, the sweet scent only intensified the picture of her utterly glistening feminine body catching the water spray as she stood there with raised hands working the soap through her hair. He remembered the way her body had fit into his when they were dancing and he shifted uncomfortably in the seat, trying to ease a sudden rising of desire threatening to escape his tight control.

Deanna glanced at him, sensing his sudden discomfort. She tried a couple of benign subjects of conversation, but after a couple of superficial comments, they died. Maybe he was nervous about her driving. A spurt of indignation sluiced through her. He was the one who had wanted to come along. If he thought they were going to end up in the bottom of a ravine, why pretend he wanted to ride with her? Then she caught herself. *No, that wasn't it.* It wasn't her driving that had suddenly made him drop some kind of a wall between them.

At first, he'd been uptight, watching the road like people do when they are mentally driving with the person behind the wheel, but after a few miles, he had begun to look at the scenery and leave the driving to her. Then what? Why put up this distance between them when they were sitting inches from each other? His body language told her that he was ready to have the ride over as soon as possible.

''What is it?'' she asked bluntly after another long stretch of silence.

"What do you mean?"

"Why are you crowding the door on your side?"

"Am I?" he asked with pretended innocence. She was too damn perceptive. How could he explain his romantic fantasies without embarrassing them both? Now was the time for a change of subject. "I do have something to tell you. Good news."

She instantly brightened. "I could use some of that."

"I found my notebook."

"You did?"

"Yes, it wasn't really lost after all."

"Thank God. Where on earth was it?"

"You won't believe who had it. Penny."

She shot him a look of disbelief. "Penny?"

He nodded. "I know. It's a real shocker."

"But how? When?"

He laughed. "The little pixie slipped it into a bag of cookies when she was gathering them up for Hobo. She waltzed out of the room as easy as you please. While we were stewing around worrying about locks and keys, the book was safely cached away in the tree house."

"I can't believe it." A wave of relief flowed through Deanna, and she apologized to him, embarrassed that her daughter had been the thief. "I'm really sorry. It never crossed my mind that she might have taken it."

"I guess Penny has a thing for small notebooks." He waited for Deanna's reaction. Did Penny's mother know that the record book with B.D. on the cover was missing? She looked honestly puzzled.

"What makes you say that?"

"Mine wasn't the only record book that Penny had stashed away in her shoe box."

She shot a quick glance at Steve. "What are you saying? Penny took someone else's book?"

He nodded, reached into the pocket of his summer jacket and drew out the black record book.

Deanna gasped when she saw it. Her hands tightened on the wheel and she took the next curve so fast she had to jerk the car back to the center of the road. "That's Ben's," she said.

"I thought it might be. And you knew it was missing?"

She nodded. "The day before he died, Ben raised holy hell about it. He was fanatical about keeping that book in his breast pocket. He called it his 'brain trust.' I didn't know what that meant, but just assumed it had to do with hotel business."

More likely, his gambling business, thought Steve. "I'm afraid it's going to be difficult to know what kind of records he was keeping. Penny has pretty well obliterated his entries with her own scribbles and happy faces. In any case, I think we should let the sheriff have a look at it."

Deanna started to ask why, but before the question was fully formed, the answer was already there. "It has to do with Ben's illicit gambling, doesn't it?"

"I don't know, but that's a possibility. If the killer knew that his name was in Ben's record book, he'd want to get his hands on it. He might have searched Ben's body for it, but since Penny had already taken it, it wasn't in Ben's pocket when he was shot."

She bit her lower lip. "So the killer could have ransacked the offices trying to find it."

"We don't know if the two incidents are connected, but it would explain why no money or anything else was taken."

"So the sheriff will have a list of suspects if he can get the names from Ben's book."

"It would seem that way. Of course, all of this is pure speculation," he added quickly. "After all, we really don't know for sure what records Ben was keeping in his book."

"It all makes sense, though. I was a complete ninny not to know what was going on, but even blind little wives can grow up and see the light." She gave a determined lift of her chin. Never again would she trust a man the way she had Benjamin.

As they covered the last stretch of winding road that dropped down into Silver Springs, Deanna glanced at her watch. "I'll have to hurry to get Maude's order. Heaven help me if I come back without something on the list."

"If you want, I could go by the sheriff's office while you're busy."

"Good idea," she said, obviously relieved to avoid another confrontation with Janson.

"You know, though, I'm likely to throttle the guy if he suggests that we're making all this up just to keep him entertained. I don't think I can take much more of his blind prejudice."

"Nor can I," she admitted. When she let him off in front of the county building, she wished him, "Good luck. I'll meet you at the Conifer Inn down the street. We'll catch a bite to eat before we head back."

"It's a date." He winked at her. "Well, we can pretend, can't we?"

Even as she chided herself for acting like some schoolgirl, she was smiling as she drove off. Funny, how a man's wink could change a gal's whole outlook, she mused. She suddenly felt younger than she had in years, and for the moment Maude and her blasted grocery list faded into the background.

SHERIFF JANSON WAS in his office, sitting behind his desk as he had been on Steve's earlier visit, only this time he wasn't reading the paper or eating. He actually looked busy.

Steve geared up for a verbal battle with the opinionated official. At his knock, Janson waved him impatiently into the room.

"Afternoon, Sheriff," Steve greeted him, deliberately remaining standing and taking advantage of his six-foot height as he looked down at the seated lawman. "A couple of things have come to light that you should know about."

"Is that so?" Janson replied, but without any sign of his usual hair-bristling indignation. "Well, grab a chair, Doc, and let's hear what you have to say."

Steve would have preferred to remain standing, but it seemed childish to refuse the man's invitation to sit down. Obviously, Janson was in a better mood than usual.

"We found my notebook. The one that was *missing*." Steve landed heavily on that last word.

Janson settled clasped hands over his belly, and waited as if curious to see what kind of a yarn Steve was going to spin this time.

As succinctly as he could, Steve explained how Penny had taken his notebook, and where she had put it for safekeeping.

Much to Steve's surprise, Janson seemed ready and willing to accept the truth that Penny had squirreled it away in her tree house. Janson's change in attitude, however, did not include an apology to him and Deanna for his unfair accusations. He just nodded and said, "Glad the thing turned up."

When Steve brought out the black book and identified

it as Ben's, Janson jerked forward in his chair. "Well, I'll be damned," he swore as he squinted at the pages, trying his best to decipher the letters and numbers almost obliterated by Penny's black felt pen.

"Every page looks like muddy pig's tracks."

"Penny did a pretty thorough job with her scribbled notes," Steve agreed.

The sheriff leaned back in his squeaky chair. "What does Deanna have to say about what's in the book?"

Sneaky way to put the question, thought Steve, and his estimation of the sheriff's cunning went up a notch. "She recognizes the book as one he always kept with him. His 'brain trust,' he called it, and she assumed it had to do with hotel business. Since Deanna didn't know anything about her husband's gambling sideline, she's in the dark about what records Ben might have kept in it," he said pointedly.

"Hmm," Janson said thoughtfully as he rubbed his chin. "Looks like it could be a betting log, but I'll be damned if I can make out any names."

"This might explain the ransacking of the offices."

"You think somebody's after this book?"

"Could be," Steve said frankly. "That makes more sense than anything."

They talked a few more minutes and Steve left with a promise from Janson that he'd do his best to ferret out any information he could from Ben's record book.

Steve felt good about the visit. At least the man seemed to have changed his attitude where Deanna was concerned, or maybe he was just playing the "good cop" for reasons of his own.

Steve left the office and walked three blocks toward the sprawling Conifer Inn, which was set on a hill overlooking the town. As he passed the Rawhide Tavern, where he had met Roger on his first trip to Silver Springs, he was greeted by the young man himself coming out of the bar.

"Hi, Doc. Just got a call from Deanna at the garage. Guess she knew where to reach me." He gave a brash laugh as if to cover up a little self-consciousness.

Steve didn't comment on the fact that it was probably well known that Roger made the tavern a routine stop when in Silver Springs.

"Didn't see any reason to hang around that smelly place while they put a new part in the damn car, you know what I mean? They told me they might not get to it till tomorrow, but Deanna says it's ready now."

"I guess you'll be heading back then?" Steve asked.

He nodded. "Yeah. Deanna's already got the supplies and put them in the van for me to take back to the hotel." There was an obvious overtone of regret in his voice. Clearly, he'd been planning on spending the night here instead of driving back to Eagle Ridge.

At that moment a beefy-looking fellow pulled up on motorcycle in front of the bar and hailed Roger with a wave of his tattooed arm. "I heard you were sitting in tonight, Rog. I'm here to give you what-for."

Roger quickly walked over to the biker, said something in a low voice and then came back to Steve. "Hate to disappoint Big Sal, but he'll have to do his barhopping without me tonight. Well, I'd better hightail it over to the garage. See ya around, Doc." He gave him a casual salute as he walked away, heading in the opposite direction from where Steve was going.

Steve mulled over the conversation he had just heard. The biker had said "sitting in," which didn't sound like barhopping to Steve, nor did "giving him what-for."

The phrases sounded more like something to do with a poker game.

Don't jump to conclusions, he warned himself. Surely the sheriff had looked into the backgrounds of everybody who worked at the hotel. Playing cards or shooting dice didn't automatically make someone a die-hard gambler, but Steve couldn't help wondering if Roger's name could be in Ben's smeared record book.

The Conifer Inn was an attractive, rustic-looking building made of hewn logs and set in the middle of a stand of huge silver spruce trees. The interior of the inn was as attractive as the exterior, with golden knotty pine walls and a center stone fireplace that dominated the room with an open-beam, two-story ceiling. Two large rooms opened off the lobby, and Steve saw that the one on the right was filled with tables for dining, the other was a spacious lounge with a bar and a small dance floor.

Steve decided to wait for Deanna in the lounge. He knew they could both use a before-dinner drink. The day had been a challenging one for both of them. He knew he'd made the right choice when she came into the lounge and dropped wearily into a chair opposite him.

"Tell me I didn't forget anything on Maude's list."

"You didn't forget anything on Maude's list," he assured her with a smile.

"Thank you. I'll expect you to stand in front of me on the firing line if you're wrong."

"I'll do that," he promised.

After the waitress had taken her order for a strawberry daiquiri, she brushed a wayward strand of hair off her forehead and smoothed the collar of her soft paisley blouse. "I've sure set a record for shopping five stores in less than one hour."

Steve wanted to tell her that she looked lovely as always. She would have been surprised to know how much he was taken with her tousled look. Soft tendrils had escaped from her usually smooth hairstyle, making a wispy frame for her oval face and beautiful complexion. Her cheeks were faintly pink from her hurried shopping trip. There was an honest beauty about her that stirred him the way some paintings did when they touched a responsive chord within his heart.

She felt his gaze traveling over her face, and she wished she'd taken time to freshen up before coming to the table. Then she chided herself for such feminine vanity when there were so many serious things that needed her attention. "Did you get to see the sheriff?"

"Yes, and it went very well."

She leaned forward as if she hadn't heard correctly. Every time she thought about Steve handing Ben's record book to Janson, her stomach curled in a knot. "What do you mean? It went well because he didn't rant and rave that I'd kept the book hidden all this time?"

"No. As far as I could tell, he accepted my explanation that Penny was responsible for snatching both notebooks and hiding them."

"And does he think that Ben kept gambling records in that book?"

"He said it could be a betting log, but he didn't have any better luck trying to read the scribbled pages than we did. Even if Penny hadn't messed up the writing, everything could be in some kind of code. I can't believe that Ben would write out full names or anything else when it came to something as illegal as in-house gambling.''

"I never realized how good he was at keeping secrets.'' She sighed sadly, and Steve knew she had been deeply hurt by his betrayal of her trust. Steve felt a rise of fury against the man who had put the sadness in her beautiful eyes.

"I'm not very hungry and I should get back to the hotel,'' Deanna said, finishing her drink. "Susan has her instructions to fix a simple dinner and keep the children in the apartment—with the door locked. How about ordering sandwiches here in the lounge instead of going into the dining room for a full-course meal?''

"Sounds good to me,'' Steve agreed. He liked the atmosphere of the lounge with its soft stereo music and hushed murmur of voices. And more than that, he liked this chance to be with Deanna away from the hotel. More and more, he'd been experiencing a building frustration with all the obstacles that prevented him from getting to know her.

They had almost finished their simple meal when several couples moved out on the dance floor. As Deanna watched them she remembered how she'd felt the night Steve had danced with her. Even now, she could feel the sudden rise of heat that had sluiced through her. Her body would never forget the way he had moved against her, stroking her, moving her hips to the suggestive beat of the music and pressing his lips to her soft neck and cheek. She avoided looking at him as her betraying senses bombarded her with arousing stimuli.

She couldn't believe it when he was on his feet, holding out a hand to her. "We have time for one dance, don't you think?''

She knew she should refuse point-blank ever to dance

with him again. Any kind of relationship with the successful psychologist promised nothing more than a fleeting interest on his part. He would be going back to the city shortly, and that would be that.

"Maybe one dance," she heard herself saying while some inner voice muttered, *Fool*.

The music was nothing like the "dirty dancing" rhythm that had been so sexually arousing the last time they'd danced. She was relieved as she moved into a smooth two-step with him, and for a minute or two she was lulled into thinking that being in his arms was going to be a harmless dancing pleasure.

Then reality set in. As he held her close, swaying to the music, pressing his cheek against hers, she knew that neither the tempo of the music nor the simplicity of the dance steps was going to change the way her senses were bombarded by his body brushing against hers. *I should make some excuse and get off the dance floor.* But as he drew her closer into the cradle of his arms, her common sense lied to her. *There isn't any harm in just one dance.*

They didn't talk. There was no need. The harmonious movement of their bodies was sensual communication enough.

One song ended. And another began.

Steve felt her submission to the rising hunger between them. A man knew things like that. The soft silk of her blouse did little to hide the teasing nipples of her breasts. He sensed that the heat flowing through his veins matched hers. An exciting desire radiated between them. He was about to kiss her when he looked into her accepting, uplifted face and came to himself with a start.

No, don't do this. She's too vulnerable. He wasn't certain enough of his own feelings to chart a steady course toward a committed relationship, and anything less than that was out of the question as far as he was concerned. He'd successfully avoided deep waters in his infrequent dating spells, and was content with the memories of a woman he'd loved so completely. Until now, he hadn't been drawn to any woman the way he was to Deanna, and that was reason enough to keep his masculine hormones under control.

Deanna felt his withdrawal. Even though he still cradled her in his arms, she sensed the change in him. No longer was he relating to her in the same charged way.

At the end of the song, his polished, easygoing manner was back. "Dancing with you could be addictive." He smiled and added, "Maybe we should be getting on our way."

Deanna accepted his smile for the brush-off that it was. Apparently whatever had been happening on the dance floor was not to his liking. *And not to mine, either,* she thought as she led the way out of the lounge.

She felt as if someone had just dropped her from a dizzying height. Her body was still floating, and tingling with unfulfilled desire. It didn't help matters to see how casual Steve was acting about the whole thing. Apparently making love on the dance floor was a common happening where he came from and she was furious with herself for being so naive.

She glanced at her watch. "I didn't intend to be gone this long. I hope Roger made it back all right with the supplies. Time for a new van, I guess."

She was glad to have something else to think about. Sometimes when her heart was full, she talked too much to relieve the tension. She led Steve into a discussion of the best kind of car for mountain deliveries, while her mind was still centered on the way her body had lusted after his on the dance floor.

Steve knew that he'd handled things badly. If his own emotions hadn't been engaged, he would have been able to play along with the situation and then put an end to it without giving her the wrong idea. Several times he started to explain himself, but his cautious nature told him he'd done enough damage for one night.

Conversation was spotty on the drive back to Eagle Ridge. Neither of them seemed able to find a neutral subject that would allow them to regain their earlier comfortable companionship. The children were the safest topic, but even that led to a discussion of his professional relationship with Penny, and was a reminder that the arrangement between them was a business one.

When they arrived back at the hotel, Deanna's manner was brisk and efficient, and all traces of the passionate woman who had melted in his arms was gone.

As they stepped out of the car at the side of the hotel, she said, "I need to double-check and see if Roger has gotten back with the supplies. Will you tell Susan when you collect Travis that I'll be along directly?"

Steve hated the brittle tone in her voice, and he knew that nothing would be served by ignoring it. "Deanna, I know I've handled things badly."

"What things? It sounds as if you did a good job with Janson. I really appreciate your handling that."

"That isn't what I'm talking about. I want to explain," he began, but a movement out of the corner of his eye stopped him. Someone was coming toward them out of the shadows. For a minute he couldn't tell who it was, and then Bob Henderson came into view.

"I thought it was about time you were getting here," he said to Deanna. "I was worried. Roger was back a couple of hours ago. I don't like you driving that pass at night." He frowned at Steve. "You didn't try driving it for the first time tonight, did you?"

"I drove," Deanna said shortly. "We decided to have a bite to eat before heading back. And now, I've had enough challenges for one day. Excuse me, gentlemen." She turned on her heel and left them standing there.

"She's riled up," Bob said accusingly. "What's going on between you two?"

"Nothing," answered Steve. *More's the pity.* "Nothing at all."

Chapter Fourteen

The last week in June was the date that Steve had set for Travis and him to return to Denver. Although he would have preferred to continue the daily sessions with Penny, he couldn't remain at the hotel indefinitely. He knew that only seeing Penny once a week when Deanna brought her to Denver for a session would slow down the little girl's progress. She was beginning to initiate some conversation now, and was showing some independent action, but he had his career to consider, as well as the need to get Travis settled in their new home.

When he talked to Deanna about his concerns, he presented her with an alternative to making a weekly trip from Eagle Ridge to Denver for Penny's sessions. "Why don't you give yourself a break from all pressures here, Dee, and spend a few weeks in Denver? Not only would it allow us to continue Penny's daily sessions, but the rest and relaxation would do you good. What do you think?"

"What do I think?" She was sitting at her desk trying to organize next month's reservations into some kind of manageable format. "You have to be kidding."

His assumption that she could just pack a couple of bags and make a jaunt into the city for a month's

R & R was almost laughable. More important than that, she knew with dead certainty that it was time to get Dr. Steve Sherman out of her personal life. He was becoming an obsession with her. Her concentration on business during the day was affected because she was thinking about him, and at night she wrestled with dreams that left her frustrated and disheartened.

He had successfully destroyed the protective cocoon she'd placed around her emotions. Now she knew what it was like to tremble in a man's arms, to feel the heat of his body, and the rising ache of passionate hunger. Running off to Denver, where he might or might not have time for her company once he was drawn back into his own social circle, would be the height of torture. "I can't possibly leave. It's out of the question."

"Don't you think it might be wise to get away from here until the sheriff makes an arrest?"

"And how long will that be?" she asked pointedly.

Steve knew he didn't have an answer. It had already been five months since her husband's death, and even though Janson's discovery of the illegal gambling might prove the key to the killer's identity, there was no guarantee that an arrest would be made soon.

"I know you have to get back to your practice," Deanna assured him, clearly dismissing him from any further obligation to remain in Eagle Ridge. "Penny has made wonderful progress overcoming the trauma of her father's death, and I'm eternally grateful. You can be sure that I'll bring her in weekly for her sessions."

So that's that. Here's your hat and here's the door. Steve didn't know whether to laugh or chide her for treating him like some guest that had overstayed his welcome. He couldn't sense any regret on her part that only a few days remained of his stay in Eagle Ridge.

Ever since their trip to Silver Springs, she'd made certain that there was no casual contact between them. He had begun to think that he'd been wrong about the magnetic sexual tension that he'd felt radiating between them on the dance floor. Had he projected his own attraction for her into something that had never been there? She certainly wasn't demonstrating any personal regrets about his leaving. He was her daughter's therapist   and that seemed to be that.

Unexpectedly, their stay at the hotel was extended a few days longer because of Silver Springs' Rodeo and Fair. Travis brought him a flyer about the Fourth of July celebration that someone had been distributing around the hotel.

"Can we go, Dad? Can we? There are going to be lots of horses and clowns and everything." His eyes flashed with excitement.

"Sorry, son. We're due back in Denver by this weekend. Our arrangement with Penny's mom was just to stay the month of June."

"But we can stay longer," Travis argued. "Dee won't mind. And Penny will want to come, too. There's even going to be a parade," he added as if his dad couldn't possibly ignore such a wonderful thing as a parade with horses and clowns.

Steve's mind veered off in a little different direction than his son's, but the idea of staying through the Fourth appealed to him, too. He was reluctant to leave until he and Deanna recovered some of the comfortable friendship that had been there off and on during his stay.

"I'll talk with Penny's mom, and see what she thinks of the idea. But don't get your hopes up."

"Why not? Aren't you always saying it's just as easy to expect the best as the worst?"

Steve laughed. Never tell a kid anything that you don't want to come back at you.

DEANNA'S REACTION was mixed when he handed her the flyer, and told her about Travis's enthusiasm for the outing. She wanted to believe that once Steve was back in Denver, she would be able to put him out of her mind,

"It's always a fun time," she agreed rather reluctantly. Seeing Steve and Travis every day had become a habit that was going to be hard to break, and putting off their departure a few more days appealed to her. "If the kids want to go, I'm agreeable."

"Good. It's settled then. We'll check out on the fifth."

Travis was jubilant when Steve told him they were staying over for the holiday. When he told Penny, she gave him a questioning smile. "Cotton candy?"

He laughed. "Definitely cotton candy."

The only person who was openly less than pleased about the delayed departure was Bob. Steve stopped at the front desk to tell him that he wouldn't be checking out that weekend. "We'll be here through the Fourth."

"I thought the arrangement Deanna made with you was free accommodation for the month of June. You, of course, will want to assume the charges for the additional days. But then—" he gave Steve a false smile "—I'm sure your professional fees will more than compensate for the minor expenses."

Steve clenched his fists to keep from hitting the officious manager right in his wide nose. Steve had waived his professional fees and had every intention of paying for the room that he and Travis had occupied. "Why don't we settle up as soon as you have the total

bill ready? Here's my credit card to cover everything—
and I mean everything. A month's lodging, meals and
any extras you can think of. I don't think Deanna will
go for my paying rental on the playroom, but if you
think you can slip it past her, go ahead.''

Color surged into Bob's broad face. His attempt to
make Steve look cheap had obviously backfired. ''It's
my job to protect Deanna from anyone taking advantage
of her. Not only in business, but in every other way,
too! I don't like what I've been seeing, Doctor.'' He
landed on the title with a kind of snarl. ''I think you've
overstayed your welcome on several accounts.''

The fierceness of his glare reminded Steve of an attack dog just watching for the right moment to go for
the throat. ''I'm sorry you feel that way, Bob. I think
we both want what is best for Deanna. I feel very protective about her myself.'' His tone registered a warning. ''Very protective.''

''You city guys like to throw your weight around,
don't you?''

''Only when there seems to be a need,'' Steve answered smoothly. He felt the manager's eyes burning
into his back as he walked away.

DEANNA ARRANGED to be away from the hotel for the
whole day, so they arrived in Silver Springs in time for
the ten o'clock parade. They found a spot near the Conifer Inn where Penny and Travis could sit on the curb
and watch while Steve and Deanna stood behind them.

Travis was like a wired jack-in-the-box, jumping up
and down, waving at people on the floats and looking
wide-eyed at horse-drawn carriages and prancing
horses. As the little boy bounced around beside Penny,

she nodded and waved along with him as the colorful parade moved by them.

Watching her daughter respond to the things going on around her was like sun breaking through dark clouds for Deanna, and she felt as if the two of them had been given a miraculous new chance at life.

"This was a wonderful idea," she told Steve.

"Yes, wasn't it?" he responded with a smile of his own. There was no denying the warm glow in her eyes, nor the way her lovely mouth softened with an appealing smile. She wore a simple yellow sundress, gathered at the waist, with a short skirt falling in soft folds over her slender hips. Her long legs were tanned, and her white open-toe sandals showed a hint of polished toenails. If she had set out to disturb him with her desirable femininity, she had succeeded, he thought, totally aware of her as the excitement and energy of the crowd surrounded them.

The parade was nearing an end when a clown with wild hair and a grotesquely painted face suddenly bounded toward Travis and Penny, laughing and blowing a raucous horn. As he flung a handful of candy at her and Travis, Penny screamed, threw herself backward away from the laughing clown. She clutched at Deanna like someone clinging to a lifesaver.

"It's all right, honey," Deanna soothed her. "He's a nice clown. He didn't mean to frighten you," she said as she comforted the little girl in her arms.

Steve was relieved when Penny accepted her mother's reassurance, and after a few minutes went back to sit on the curb beside Travis. *Thank heavens! No harm done. Just the normal fright of a child when something scares them.* Penny had come a long way in the month he'd been working with her. She was able to handle the unexpected now without retreating into her protective shell.

"Here, Penny." Travis gave her some of the candy he'd quickly picked up. "It's a good kind. Tootsie Rolls."

Deanna started to say something about spoiling their lunch but gave up worrying about such mundane things. This was a holiday. Their first outing for months.

"What now?" Steve asked after the last horse and buggy had gone by.

"Now we go to the fairgrounds."

Steve was surprised at the number of exhibition buildings where a variety of entries were being judged. He'd never been to a county fair, and he was surprised at the different kinds of exhibits and booths that lined the midway.

"Do you want to enter the watermelon seed–spitting contest, Steve?" Deanna teased.

"I think I'll pass on that one."

Travis was a lot more interested in the judging of 4-H animals than he was in ribbon winners in quilts, garden flowers, and canned and baked goods. The boy bounced all over the place, looking at goats, ducks, chickens and even some llamas.

They had a hard time dragging Travis away from the horse barn, and when they came to a petting zoo, all was lost until he had touched all the baby rabbits, lambs and little pink pigs.

"Come on, Penny," Travis urged. "This is a nice little bunny. I bet his name is Peter Rabbit just like in your book."

"Peter Rabbit?" Penny surprised Steve by looking up at him for confirmation.

"That's a nice name for a bunny rabbit," he said

evasively. He wasn't going to gamble with Penny's trust in him by pretending that this was indeed *the* Peter Rabbit. "He looks like the one in your book, doesn't he? He has the same brown and white spots."

Apparently this response satisfied Penny because she sat down on a bench and let Travis put the bunny in her lap. Very tenderly she stroked the rabbit's soft fur, and a peace that was almost angelic touched her little face.

Deanna's hand unwillingly crept into Steve's as they watched the child open up to the love of the small bunny. He'd never felt so close to her as he did at that moment when she gave his hand a grateful squeeze and looked at him with misty eyes. "How can I ever thank you?" she said.

"You always have." He wanted to tell her that this past month had been the happiest he'd known since his wife's death, but she purposefully withdrew her hand from his, and the moment passed.

After lunch, they spent the afternoon sitting high in the grandstand watching cowboys race quarter horses, rope calves on the run and get pitched off of ferocious Brahman bulls as they tried to ride them. They yelled, clapped and ate junk food.

As the rodeo ended, the crowd began to pour out of the grandstand as all the livestock were being returned to their pens and the center area was being cleared for the country music performers later that evening.

As they exited the grandstand, vendors were all over the place selling balloons, banners and other souvenirs. A cotton-candy booth caught Penny's attention, and she jerked away from Deanna's hand and headed straight for it as fast as she could go.

"Wait up, Penny," Deanna ordered, but the child

continued to dart through a swarm of people between her and the candy booth.

"I'll get her." Steve kept his eyes on the fleeting glimpse of her tousled yellow hair as he shoved his way through the milling crowd, but before he could reach her, a couple of horseback riders slowed his stride, and when they'd passed, Penny was nowhere to be seen.

"Penny! Penny!" he shouted, his anxious eyes darting in every direction.

Where had she gone?

It was a miracle that in the cacophony of voices, carnival noises and laughter, he heard her terrified cry. He swung around in that direction and shouted, "Stop! Stop!"

A masked, redheaded clown was just disappearing around the corner of the animal sheds and corrals with Penny clutched harshly to his chest. Steve bolted through the crowd, roughly shoving people aside in his mad run after Penny and her abductor.

A maze of corrals held animals used in the various rodeo events, and as Steve came around the corner, he saw the clown reach over one of the fences and drop Penny inside an empty corral. Steve nearly overtook him as he darted away through the animal pens, but a bunch of horses being herded into a corral separated them, and by the time they'd passed, Steve had lost sight of the clown.

Steve swore as he raced back to the corral where the clown had dropped Penny. He was surprised to see that Travis was already there.

"No, Travis!" Steve shouted when he saw that his son was climbing over the high corral fence to get to Penny.

The boy gave no indication that he'd heard, threw his

leg over the high railing and scrambled down board by board until he nimbly dropped down beside the sobbing little girl.

Deanna was only a few steps behind Travis but not close enough to stop him. When she let out a terrified scream, Steve didn't know what was happening.

"Look!" she cried.

When he followed the frantic waving of her arm, his whole body froze. At the far end of the corral, fierce Brahman bulls that were being returned from the rodeo area were pouring in through an open gate. The cowboys herding them did not see the two children huddle on the ground in the path of the trampling animals.

With a dexterity born of pure panic, Steve climbed over the high corral railing and dropped down by the children. Their nostrils had begun to fill from the dust of the heavy-footed, trampling animals.

Grabbing Travis by the shoulders, Steve shoved him toward the fence. "Climb!"

Travis looked back at Penny.

"I'll get her. Move! Now!"

Obeying his father's order, Travis scrambled up the log railings and over the top, and would have fallen to the ground on the other side if Deanna hadn't caught him.

Steve turned to pick up Penny, but before he had her in his arms, a package of lighted firecrackers came sailing through the air and landed a few feet from him.

"What the—?" He lurched toward the smoking fireworks, but he was too late to smother the fuse.

The first firecracker went off.

Steve was so close that his face was hotly seared from the burnt powder, but the pain scarcely touched his consciousness. A chain reaction in the bundle of lighted firecrackers sounded like machine-gun fire.

In an instant the rapid explosions stampeded the bulls.

Blinded by the rising dust, Steve frantically reached out for Penny and pulled her into his arms. Pressed against the fence with the roar of churning animals all around him, he managed to lift the child up over his head.

"Climb, Penny. Climb."

She grabbed one of the railings with her little hands, and with Steve pushing her up, she made it over the top railing, and fell into the arms of her mother.

"Hurry, Dad!" Travis shouted.

"Get out," Deanna pleaded frantically.

He could hear them calling to him, but his eyes were smarting too badly to see anything. His face was on fire from the burn of the firecrackers.

He pressed up against the corral fence as a snorting bull brushed into him and nearly dragged him into the sea of trampling hooves before he could gain any foothold on the rails of the corral. When his pant leg was snagged by one of the bull's horns, he was nearly dragged into the cauldron of trampling feet. Struggling to keep his footing as he climbed upward, he lifted himself out of the sea of animals, flung himself over the top railing and dropped down on the other side.

"Thank God," Deanna breathed as he stood in front of her, his face blackened and red from the exploding firecrackers.

"You okay, Dad?" Travis asked anxiously.

A crowd had begun to gather. One of the cowboys who had been herding the bulls into the pen and who'd seen what happened, muttered, "Damn fools."

Steve ignored his remarks and demanded, ''Where's the nearest telephone? We need to alert the authorities.''

''Under the grandstand. What are you going to do? Blame somebody else for wandering around where you folks had no business to be?''

Instead of answering him, Steve turned to the crowd that had collected around them. Most of them were horsemen or hired hands to handle the rodeo animals. ''Did any of you see a redheaded clown running through here? Or throwing firecrackers into the bull pen?''

Nobody had. Either they were cautious about offering any information or hadn't seen anything. Steve knew he didn't have time to waste. Every minute counted when it came to finding the abductor.

He was about to turn away, when one of the gawkers pointed. ''Here comes Pete Hawkins. He's in charge of rodeo security.''

''What's going on here?'' the potbellied man wearing boots and spurs demanded as he reached them. ''Somebody said some kids were playing in the bull corral. You the parents?'' he demanded, scowling at Steve and Deanna. ''Can't you keep better track of your younguns than that?''

Steve managed to keep his temper in check and drew the man aside so that he could talk without Penny hearing. He explained as simply and clearly as he could that the little girl had been snatched near the cotton-candy booth by a man in a red wig, wearing a mask and dressed in a clown's suit.

''When I chased him, he dumped her in the bull pen, and before I could get her out, he threw in some lighted firecrackers to stampede the animals. I made a dash for the firecrackers when they went off.''

Steve's red and slightly blackened face left little doubt that he was telling the truth.

Hawkins swung around and gave an order to the men collected there, "Fan out and look for a clown wearing a red wig and face mask. Don't let him get away." Then he pulled out a walkie-talkie and began alerting security officers all over the park.

"Will they catch him, Dad?" Travis asked anxiously.

"He couldn't have gotten away from the fairgrounds this fast. Someone's bound to notice him," Steve said, but his optimism was short-lived.

In less than five minutes, one of the searchers returned, carrying a clown suit, wig and mask. "I found these dumped behind one of the exhibition buildings. I guess we're not looking for a clown anymore."

Steve and Deanna exchanged worried looks.

Whoever had worn the clown costume could now pass through the crowd unnoticed.

Chapter Fifteen

The manager of the Conifer Inn was acquainted with Deanna, and he was more than solicitous when she told him that they had decided to spend the night in Silver Springs rather than driving back to Eagle Ridge to her own hotel.

"Because of the celebration, we are booked solid, but you're in luck. We've had one unexpected cancellation."

"We'll take it," Steve said readily.

The manager glanced at him and Deanna, and then at the two children. His thoughts were easy to read. He was obviously wondering what kind of relationship this might be. "It's a room with two double beds and a small sitting room with a fold-down couch."

Deanna turned to Steve. "That will do nicely, don't you think?"

"Very nicely," he agreed, silently thanking the people who had canceled their reservation. The last hour at the fairgrounds had been a nightmare. When Sheriff Janson arrived, he took charge. They did their best to answer his questions, but they had very few answers that satisfied him.

"Yes, he was a good-size man."

"No, we couldn't tell what he looked like because of the mask."

"No, he wasn't the same clown that had frightened Penny at the parade."

"No, we hadn't seen him before. He wasn't one of the rodeo clowns who had been in the arena during the bull-riding event."

When Janson finally quit asking questions, very little progress had been made toward finding the abductor. He told them to stay in Silver Springs while he did some more investigating.

By the time they checked in at the inn, all of them were exhausted. Steve looked like a fugitive from a war zone. Unlike his usual rambunctious self, Travis's steps were dragging, and Penny was so drained of energy that Steve ended up carrying her up to the room.

As he laid the little girl down on one of the double beds, she startled him by putting her arms around his neck. Looking at him with tired but clear eyes, she whispered, "Love you."

He swallowed hard. As he tenderly brushed back the hair from her dusty face, he wanted to shout with joy. The horrid experience had not sent her back into her withdrawal state. "Love you, too, sweetheart."

As Deanna watched the tender scene between Steve and her daughter, she blinked rapidly to keep tears from spilling out of the corners of her eyes. She had been prepared for the worst possible reaction from Penny, and she couldn't believe that her daughter was handling the near tragedy even better than she.

"Do you think we can get these two in and out of the shower before they fall asleep on us?" Steve asked her as Travis came trudging into the room.

"Which bed's mine?" the boy demanded with tired

pugnaciousness. His clothes were rumpled, and his face was smeared with dust.

"I don't think we've decided," Steve answered smoothly. "What do you think, Dee? Can you and Penny share a bed?"

"Yes, of course." *Did that mean that he and Travis would take the other one?*

He smiled as if he was aware of her unspoken question. "Then Travis can have the other bed, and I'll take the couch."

She wanted to protest that there was no need for him to sleep in the other room, but she knew better than to lie to herself—and to him. He'd haunted her dreams when he'd been sleeping in a room on a different floor. How could she lie in the next bed, close enough to reach out and touch him, and not be aware of every breath he drew?

"All right, troops. Who's first into the shower?" Steve asked, taking charge of the weary little group.

Deanna was glad for the bustle of getting Penny and Travis cleaned up and put to bed. She took a long time in the shower, and Steve teased her about using all the hot water before he got his.

Before coming to the inn, they'd stopped at a clothing store and drugstore to pick up a simple change of clothing for all of them—shorts, tops, underwear and some toiletries. The kids were sleeping in their underwear, and after their showers, Deanna wore a white terry-cloth robe provided by the inn, and he put on a pair of jeans and no shirt.

Steve wondered if she was planning on sleeping in the nude. When she helped him make up his sofa bed, the graceful movement of her body under the short robe was mesmerizing. As she stretched her arms to smooth out a sheet, the fullness of her breasts created a plunging neckline and revealed soft warm skin just waiting to be traced with butterfly kisses. He had to force his gaze away from the tempting view of her derriere as she bent over the bed to straighten out a cover. With difficulty, he restrained a playful desire to loosen the belt on her robe.

"There, that should do it," she said as she stepped back and viewed the sofa bed. "If you want to sleep with Travis, I would be perfectly comfortable here."

"No, this'll be fine."

A huskiness in his voice made her turn around and look at him. His eyes were warm with masculine interest. Instinctively, her hands went to the opening of the robe and she pulled it tighter.

He saw the gesture and collected himself. The circumstances were difficult enough for her to handle without adding to them. "Listen, I know this forced intimacy isn't easy for you. I'll do my best to keep things on a sane level."

With mixed feelings, she realized that once more he had put a safe sexual distance between them. In one way she was glad, but at a deeper level she felt cheated. *It's your own fault. Why'd you have to act all prissy because you caught him looking at you?*

There was a professional edge to his voice as he said, "If you're not too tired, I think we should talk about what happened today."

"Do we have to?"

"I think so. Even though it's tempting to try and block out the horror, it's better in the long run to verbalize feelings rather than trying to cover them up."

"I suppose you're right." She sat down on the edge

of the bed. "At the moment I'm so drained, I don't know how I feel."

He threaded his slightly damp hair with his fingers. "I have to admit that my anger and frustration is at a flashpoint. I want to lash out at somebody. Dammit, enough is enough!"

Nodding wearily, she resisted the temptation to cover her face with her hands and have a good cry. Those torturing minutes when Penny, Travis and Steve's very lives had been in jeopardy would be with her for as long as she lived. Her stomach tightened just remembering the exploding firecrackers and swirls of dust from the stampeding bulls, when those minutes of terrifying horror had been an agonizing eternity.

He took one look at her pale face and said, "I think we both could do with a drink." He picked up the phone and called room service. He put his hand over the receiver and asked, "None of us ate much dinner. Would you like me to order something to eat, too?"

She shook her head. "Brandy sounds good. But I don't think I could handle food."

Outside their windows, the sound of firecrackers and the shooting glare of rockets heralded the evening's activities. It was hard for Deanna to remember that other people were enjoying a normal, happy holiday. She wanted to block out the noise, the gaiety and the promise that life for some people could be sane and wonderful.

"Who would be so heartless?" she asked as they sipped their drinks a while later.

"The same person who would try and poison a little girl," he answered curtly.

"Then you think it's the same person? Sheriff Janson

gave the impression that he thought the two acts might be unrelated.''

''Give me a break!'' Steve scoffed, wanting to kick something. The sheriff's bullheadedness was infuriating. ''The whole abduction thing had to be premeditated. Someone knew we'd be at the fairgrounds.''

''But who?''

''Everyone at the hotel, for starters. Anyone could have called the hotel and been told that all of us were in Silver Springs. We were at the parade and fair for more than six hours before Penny was snatched. Plenty of time for someone to catch up with us.''

But who? They were back to the same question. The impact of all the stress she'd endured during the day suddenly seemed like a weight too heavy to carry a moment longer.

''I think I'll say good-night,'' she said wearily. She stood up and started to brush by him.

''Deanna.'' He stopped her with a gentle hand on her arm. The way he'd said her name was like a soft caress, and every nerve in her body was suddenly awakened by the way he was looking at her. Her heart quickened. Since her devastating surrender to the sexual hunger so evident as they'd danced together, her imagination had worked overtime on all the seductive things he might say to her in a raw sweep of desire.

He said softly, ''I want you to know that you are the most remarkable woman I've ever met.''

Remarkable? *Remarkable?* She turned the word over in her mind as a kind of hysterical laughter caught in her throat. Not devastating. Not appealing. Not sexy. Not charming. Just remarkable. She felt like a civic-minded citizen who'd just been awarded a paper certificate. This definitely wasn't the kind of compliment she'd hoped for from a man who had turned her romantic fantasies upside down.

She managed a brittle false smile. "And I think you're very upstanding, Dr. Sherman."

"Upstanding?" he echoed.

"Yes, very upstanding." *Two could play this game.* "And I admire you because you're ethical, and principled, and honorable, and—"

She never finished because in one swift movement he pulled her to him and his mouth came down on hers and shut off her breath with a long, questing kiss. None of her wildest imaginings had prepared her for the sensations that poured through her. As he cradled her against the muscular length of his body, everything she'd ever known about making love was swept away. She put her arms around his neck, and the breathless kiss deepened as his tongue began to tease the sweetness of her mouth.

The pressure of her breasts and thighs fired a wild hunger in Steve that had lain dormant for much too long. His feelings for her had gone beyond just the momentary pleasure of being with her this last month, and certainly beyond the traumatic circumstances that had thrown them together. He'd been a fool to think that he could put her out of his life. He lifted his mouth from her moist lips and broke the heated kiss.

He whispered, "If you don't go in the bedroom and shut the door, my principles and ethics are going to be a thing of the past."

"Is that a promise?" she teased, her breath uneven.

"More than that. It's a certainty."

Outside, the rockets were bursting with fiery sprays of stars, and when he kissed her once more with fervent intent, she felt them exploding in her own heart. His hands found their way under the robe, and she made no protest as the belt fell away and his hands caressed her with impelling urgency. He was about to lower her back on the bed, when a child's loud cry stopped them.

Penny!

They pulled apart, and Steve quickly opened the bedroom door. Deanna rushed past him. The little girl was sitting straight up in bed, wide-eyed and sobbing, "Mommy. Mommy." Then she pointed to a shadowy corner of the room. "Bad man. Bad man."

"It's all right, honey. It's all right," Deanna soothed, cradling and rocking the child in her arms.

Steve quickly turned on the overhead light. "See, Penny. There's no bad man here."

She looked around the room with rounded, tearful eyes, and then turned her face into her mother's chest, her little shoulders shaking with sobs.

Travis sat up. "What's the matter with Penny?"

"She had a bad dream."

Travis looked at Penny's mother cuddling her. "Me, too," he said as if this was too good an opportunity to pass up. "Can I sleep with you, Dad?"

"Sure. Why not?" He sent Deanna a regretful smile. "Not exactly what I had in mind. We'll see you ladies in the morning."

STEVE LAY AWAKE listening to the rhythmic breathing of his son. Even when a loneliness had engulfed him after Carol's death, he'd always been in control of his feelings. There had been plenty of chances to bring a woman permanently into his life again. Some of them would have been a good mother for Travis, but he hadn't been in love with any of them, and he doubted that they had been more than infatuated with him. Was

Deanna confusing gratitude with love? He needed to be honest with himself and with Deanna, and that was the problem. He didn't know what the truth between them really was.

The Fourth of July racket went on most of the night and Steve was sure he'd just fallen asleep when the telephone rang in the room at five o'clock in the morning.

"What the—?"

Grabbing for the phone, he nearly knocked it off the small table by the sofa before he barked a hoarse, "Hello."

"Is this room 207?" It was a man's voice.

There was a long pause while Steve searched his memory for the room number. Travis stirred but didn't wake up.

"Yes, it's 207," Steve grumbled.

"Who is this?" the ungracious voice demanded.

"Steve Sherman. And who is this calling at five o'clock in the morning?"

"Bob Henderson," was the curt answer. "Where's Deanna? They told me this was her room."

"Oh, it is," Steve answered, giving in to an urge to taunt the pompous manager. He spoke softly so he wouldn't wake up Travis, but the jealous man on the other end of the line didn't know that. "But she's still asleep."

"Well, wake her up," Bob growled. "I have to talk with her."

"What's so important that it can't wait a couple of hours?"

"None of your damn business. Now put Deanna on the phone!"

Steve might have given in to the impulse to hang up

on the irate man, but the door between their rooms opened and Deanna looked at him questioningly. Apprehension was back in her face, and he could tell from the lavender shadows under her eyes that she hadn't gotten any more sleep than he had.

"Who is it?"

"Your ever-loving manager."

"Bob? At this hour?"

"The one and only." He handed her the phone.

Moving as far away from the sofa bed as the cord of the phone would allow, she said quietly, "Yes, Bob, what is it?"

Steve watched her profile as she listened. The muscles in her face became rigid. Color drained from her face. Just looking at her, he felt his own chest muscles tighten.

"Oh my God." She clutched the phone to her ear with a white-knuckled hand. Raw horror was on her face.

Steve was out of bed and at her side in an instant, forgetting that he was clad only in undershorts. He wanted to take the phone and find out for himself what the shattering news was that Bob had given her, and it was pure torture to restrain himself.

"Where is she now?" Deanna listened, and after another long moment said, "All right. I'll get right over there. Yes, I'll call you as soon as I find out anything." She hung up without even saying goodbye.

"What is it? What's happened?"

Deanna opened her mouth to answer but no words came out. It was as if the connection between her brain and vocal cords had been severed. After all that had happened, she had thought she was immune to paralyzing shock. Now her body felt numb and her thoughts were like cotton, without form and body.

Steve took her by the shoulders and gave her a firm shake. "Tell me."

Her thick lips mouthed the words, "It's Susan. She's in a coma. She may die."

"A coma?" he echoed. "What happened?"

"Last night, someone…someone attacked her," she stammered. With halting breath she told him what Bob had said. "She was at Corky's Café with Jeffery. They had a fight. Susan stalked out of the place. The parking lot was crowded, and when Jeffery went after her, he couldn't find her right away until he heard her scream. When he found her, she was unconscious from a blow to the head. Whoever did it got away while Jeffery brought her inside the café and called an ambulance."

"Where is she now?"

"Here in Silver Springs. It's the closest hospital to Eagle Ridge. I've got to get over there right away. Bob said they weren't sure she would make it through the night. Will you see to Penny?"

He nodded, pulled her close and touched a kiss to her forehead. Then he tipped up her brave chin, and looked straight into her eyes. "I'll be here as long as you need me. You're not in this thing alone."

As he held her for a long minute, renewed strength flowed into her body. The passion of the night before was replaced with a blending of spirits that promised a wholeness she had never experienced before. Even though she knew better, she had fallen in love with this man. She wanted to tell him how she felt, but she feared that he would dismiss her feelings as emotion wrought by the urgency of the moment.

He walked with her to the door. "Call me as soon as you know anything."

SILVER SPRINGS Community Hospital was a modest brick building at the west end of town, and when Deanna entered the small waiting room on the second floor, she saw that Susan's parents were already there. Mr. and Mrs. Whitcomb were ranchers who had a small spread up the river valley. Deanna had met them several times during the summer when they visited Susan on her day off, and she liked them both. Her heart went out to them when she saw how the all-night vigil at their daughter's side had taken its toll.

"I'm so terribly sorry. How is she?" Deanna asked anxiously.

"No change," Mrs. Whitcomb told her, wadding up a damp tissue.

"She's holding her own." Susan's father's words had the force of his own stubborn determination. "Doc says she's putting up a fight."

"Who would want to hurt my little girl?" Susan's mother asked tearfully.

"Some damn drunk, that's who," Mr. Whitcomb swore. "Some low-down skunk of a man who can't keep his hands off a pretty girl."

"They only let us in to see Susan ten minutes every hour," complained her mother.

As they waited for some news about Susan, Deanna tried to put a leash on her own thoughts because they kept leading her into a quagmire of questions. Was the attack on Susan a separate act of violence? Did it have anything to do with Ben's death and the danger to Penny? Was it just a coincidence? Or was the assault tied in some way to the nightmare that had engulfed her life?

She shouldn't have been surprised when Sheriff Janson walked into the waiting room, but she was. Just his presence triggered all the thoughts she had been struggling to keep separate from the present situation. Did the sheriff think there was a connection? Is that why he was here?

Obviously Janson knew the Whitcombs. He nodded at Mrs. Whitcomb and gave Susan's father a brisk pat on the back. "How's your girl, Elmer?"

"She's holding her own," Mr. Whitcomb repeated with the same stubbornness with which he'd answered Deanna.

Janson took off his hat and twirled it lightly in his hands as he talked to the Whitcombs. His rough exterior was softer than usual, and Deanna saw a side of him she hadn't seen before. He didn't ask any questions or make any flat statements, but he simply listened, and promised he'd do everything to catch the varmint who had hurt their daughter.

When he was ready to leave, he nodded at Deanna. "Could I see you for a few minutes, Deanna?"

She nodded, but she wasn't sure she was up to their usual verbal battles.

After taking the elevator downstairs, they walked out to the front of the building before he said anything. He led the way over to a bench that was set to one side of the entrance. "Have a seat."

She sat down, her palms sweaty, the cords in her neck tight with tension. Somehow she knew that what he was about to say wasn't going to clear up anything. Rather than waiting for him to say what was on his mind, she plunged in. "Do you know who might have done this to Susan?"

"No. Do you?" he asked in his usual accusing tone.

She blinked. "Is that why you brought me out here? To somehow twist the blame for this onto me?"

"I'm just looking for some answers. Have you got any for me?"

"If I did, I certainly wouldn't play cat and mouse with you. Susan means too much to me. I'll do anything I can to help find the animal who did this."

Janson pulled out a toothpick and started chewing on it. "I was wondering if it could be a lover's quarrel."

Deanna thought she wasn't hearing correctly. "A lover's quarrel?" Deanna's mind raced ahead. Bob had said that Susan stomped out of the restaurant because she and Jeffery had had a fight. Could the young man have followed her out and made up the story about someone else striking her? "You think Jeffery is lying about what happened?"

"No, his story seems to hold together. I was thinking about Roger."

"Roger?"

"I hear he and Susan have been pairing off now and again. Since this happened, Jeffery has been making loud noises that we should be pulling Roger in for questioning. Of course, the young man's as green with jealousy as a ripe cucumber. I guess that's what the fight at the café was about."

"But why would Roger want to hurt Susan?"

He shifted the toothpick in his mouth. "I was thinking that maybe you'd have an idea, being a woman with men fighting over her and all."

"Nobody's fighting over me."

"You've always been pretty good at lying to yourself, Deanna. You thought you had a good marriage with that older fellow of yours, but everybody else knew differently.'' He eyed her. ''I think you've grown up a lot of late, gal.''

She responded to a hint of his smile. ''Yes, I have. And I agree that I should have kept my eyes open a little wider.'' She summoned her courage and asked the questions that had been like a swarm of bees tormenting her. ''Do you think the assault on Susan has anything to do with Ben's murder? Is her attacker the same one who's been trying to hurt Penny?''

He broke the toothpick in half with his stubby finger and tossed it away. ''Could be.''

''Why? Why hurt Susan?''

''Effin I knew that, I wouldn't be sitting here, hoping you'll throw out a line so I can reel in a catch.'' He sighed. ''We're checking out alibis for yesterday. Because it was a holiday, people were all over the place.''

She moistened her dry lips. ''No guesses who the clown might have been?''

''That's about all I have. Guesses.'' He stood up. ''Well, I reckon I'm not doing any good sitting here. You'd best get back upstairs to the Whitcombs.''

''What if Susan dies?'' Her voice broke.

''And what if she doesn't?'' Deanna was startled when he reached out and clumsily patted her shoulder. ''What if Susan provides the link that ties all this together tighter than a roping knot?''

Chapter Sixteen

Deanna stayed at the hospital until midafternoon, and when there was no change in Susan's condition, she left the Whitcombs to their vigil and returned to the inn.

As she pulled into the parking lot, Steve and the two children were just returning from playing in the park a few blocks away. He raised a questioning eyebrow as Deanna came toward them. From her expression, he expected the worst, but she shook her head and said, "No change."

"Mommy, look." Penny ran to her, holding up a little monkey on a swing. Her happy smile was worth a million dollars to Deanna. "He's Jocko."

"Nice to meet you, Jocko," Deanna said solemnly.

"I got an airplane, Dee," Travis told her with his usual energetic bounce. He held up a balsa-wood airplane for her approval.

"Very nice." She was glad to see that the traumatic events of the day before had not left any visible marks on either child.

"It flies high," Travis bubbled. "Here, I'll show you." With big-boy importance he shot the balsa-wood airplane into the air with a rubber band. The plane made a half circle and landed on top of a juniper bush twice as tall as Travis. "Oops."

He sent a hopeful look at Steve.

With a chuckle, Steve retrieved the plane by giving the bush a good shake. "I'm not climbing any trees, so you'd better fly this thing closer to the ground."

"I guess I don't need to ask how you managed the kids all day," Deanna said as they made their way into the inn. She smiled at him. "It's obvious you spoiled them rotten."

"You can't spoil children by having fun with them," he countered.

"Especially when you're a kid yourself?" she teased. "I suspected as much, and now I know. Child's play is a cover-up for what you do best."

"And what is that?" His eyes sparkled almost as much as his son's.

"I haven't quite decided," she admitted honestly. He was a man who could never be defined by labels. There was depth of character in his easy smile and caring manner. She knew only too well the depth of passion in his kisses, and the way his touch filled her senses to overflowing. A woman could love a man like that all her life—if she had the chance.

"And what do you do best?" he challenged.

"Lie to myself," she said, surprising herself with her honesty.

"Maybe you need a therapist to make a truthful woman out of you."

She shot him a quick look, wondering if the facetious answer had any depth to it. She couldn't tell. As always, he was able to tread a fine line between a light casual manner and that of a professional. Maybe she would never know whether his feelings for her were only sexual chemistry, or something more. She knew he had already settled up his account at her hotel and had planned to leave Eagle Ridge that morning.

"I guess you'll be staying another day," she said as she gathered up their belongings. "It's too late now to make a drive to Denver."

"I already called the hotel and told Bob to move our stuff out of the room at checkout time."

"Oh." Her heart sank. "Then you're planning on driving back tonight?"

"No. I asked him to move all our belongings into your apartment."

"What?" She couldn't believe she'd heard him correctly. "You're moving in with me?"

"Well, not exactly. Since you won't leave Eagle Ridge, I've decided to stay close by until I feel you and Penny are safe. In this case, 'moving in with you' means that you've acquired a watchdog. Unless, of course, you might want to extend that definition to include something more?" He grinned. "I'm open to other options."

Her feelings were at once relieved, delighted, and slightly ruffled. "Don't you think you should have asked me first?"

"I was afraid the invitation might not be forthcoming," he answered honestly, and let his hands touch her bare arms in a seductive way.

"And what makes you think I won't dump your stuff in the hall and send you on your way?"

He considered the prospect seriously. "If you did that, I'd just have to set up camp outside your door. And that might raise a few eyebrows."

She smiled back. "In that case, I guess it would be better for you and Travis to take the spare room."

"We'll see." Without warning, he lowered his head and captured her mouth in a long possessive kiss.

They didn't know that Travis was standing in the bedroom doorway, watching, until he squealed, "Lookee, Penny! Dad's kissing Dee. Dad's kissing Dee."

Both children stared with wide eyes. Reluctantly, Steve set her away from him, mouthing a promise, "Later."

"Is Dee going to live with us?" Travis asked excitedly.

"As a matter of fact, we're going to live with her and Penny for a little while."

"Did you hear that, Penny?" He clapped his hands in joy. "I'm going to live with you and Hobo for a little while."

A little while. Deanna knew the arrangement was a temporary one as far as Steve was concerned, and for the moment she accepted it for the blessing that it was.

They headed back to Eagle Ridge as long shadows of dusk turned the mountainsides into soft purple-green carpets. As Deanna drove the mountain pass once more, the headlights of the car darted around the curves like a night creature in flight.

While the children entertained themselves in the back seat of the car, she quietly told Steve about Susan's attack and Janson's speculation about it. "He thinks that either Jeffery or Roger might be responsible since she's been kinda playing double-time with both of them."

Steve was thoughtful for several miles. He recalled the talk he'd had with Susan, and the few contacts he'd had with Jeffery. He'd spent more time with Roger because of their trip to Silver Springs together. As a trained psychologist, he knew that people were rarely what they seemed on the surface. Neither Jeffery nor

Roger seemed the violent type, but sometimes the most benign person hid a twisted personality.

"What do you think? Is it possible one of them assaulted Susan like that?" Deanna asked, sending a quick glance at his thoughtful expression.

"It's a possibility, of course."

"You don't sound convinced."

"I guess not."

It seemed more likely to Steve that Susan had somehow gotten crosswise of the same demented person who had been wreaking treacherous havoc on Deanna and her daughter, but he didn't want to tell her so.

"I know what you're thinking." She tightened her lips. "I've been over the same ground. There's a connection between Ben's death and what's been happening since then." Her voice wavered. "I'm sure of it."

Since she'd introduced the subject, he asked, "What time was it when Susan was hurt?"

"About midnight, Bob told me."

Plenty of time for the masked clown to make it back to Eagle Ridge. But why? Why go after Susan?

BOTH BOB AND JEFFERY were at the desk when they returned to the hotel, and almost in unison, they asked, "How's Susan?"

Deanna repeated the news again, "No change. Holding her own."

"I've got to go to the hospital to see her," Jeffery said.

"The sheriff says you're to stay away from Susan until he figures this thing out," Bob told him sharply. "There's nothing you can do for her. Right, Deanna?"

"Her parents are there, Jeffery." The young man looked as if he'd been in a torture chamber for the last twenty-four hours. "Susan's in good hands," she reassured him. "Why don't you take the night off?"

He shook his head. "I'd rather keep busy."

"I'm sorry I interrupted your Fourth of July holiday by calling so early this morning," Bob said, but his tone was more acidic than apologetic.

"No problem," said Steve smoothly. "We all went to bed rather early."

Deanna knew the impression that Steve had given, and only part of it was true. They hadn't slept together, but they'd come mighty close to it. Deanna wondered if her face looked as warm as it felt.

Bob pointedly spoke to Deanna as if Steve weren't standing there. "I wanted to check with you first, Deanna, before I had Dr. Sherman's stuff moved into your apartment, but I couldn't get hold of you. We haven't rented his room, so we can move everything back if you want."

"No, it's fine. Steve and Travis will be staying with me. Temporarily," she added.

"I see," he said icily.

Before Bob could comment any further on the arrangement, she turned to Steve. "Why don't you take the kids up to the apartment? There are probably some things in the office I need to check on."

"Sure. Come on, kids."

She'd only planned to spend a few minutes in her office, but the minutes stretched into several hours. Her desk was piled with matters that Bob assured her could not wait. By the time she got free, it was already past dinnertime, and the dining room had closed an hour earlier.

When she came in the apartment, she laughed when she saw that Steve and the children had been having an impromptu picnic in the middle of the floor. She was glad Steve had ordered up some sandwiches and drinks from the kitchen before it closed.

"We're going to Corky's Café to have chocolate malts for dessert," Travis greeted her excitedly.

Steve held out his hands in a gesture of surrender. "I tried to talk them out of it, but I was outvoted."

While Deanna was trying to decide whether or not she wanted to go, Travis bounded up, grabbed his airplane, and was halfway to the door. "Come on, Dad, you promised."

"I go, too." Penny scurried after him with Hobo at her heels. The dog was ready for an outing, and leaping around as if they'd been gone for a week instead of just overnight, even though several of the hotel staff had given him a lot of attention.

"Why don't the three of you go on," Deanna suggested.

"Have you had anything to eat?"

When she shook her head, he slipped his arm around her waist. "I'll buy you a fat hamburger to go with a chocolate malt."

The warmth of his nearness, and the way he was smiling at her made refusal impossible. Even though she'd only been back at the hotel for a couple of hours, she was already feeling weighted down by the never-ending responsibility.

"All right. A hamburger and malt, it is."

As it turned out, they didn't even make it past the main desk before Jeffery called out to her. "Wait up, Deanna. A call just came in for you. I'm not sure, but I think it may be the hospital."

Deanna spun around, "I'll take it in my office."

"I'll go with you," Steve said, fearing the news might be bad.

"Oh, Dad!" wailed Travis in protest at the delay.

"Wait right here by the desk," he ordered. "You and Penny play with your toys. We'll be back in a few minutes."

"Bummer," muttered Travis. Reluctantly, he pulled out his new airplane and began to play with it. On his first try, he sent it flying across the lobby, and through the open door of the empty dining room.

"No, Hobo, no!" Travis yelled as the dog ran after it, and he scurried to retrieve the airplane before the dog could mistake it for a game of fetch.

"Where did it go? Did you see it, Penny?" Travis looked around anxiously.

Luckily the dog got sidetracked by smells coming out of the kitchen. Hobo shoved his nose into the crack of the swinging doors, and disappeared just about the time that Travis spied his airplane on one of the dining-room chairs.

"I found it," he told Penny gleefully.

Penny pointed to the kitchen. "Get Hobo."

"Did he go in there? Stupid dog." Travis pushed his way through the doors into the kitchen. "Hobo! Hobo!"

Travis could see the dog's tail wagging near some trash cans by the back door. They reached him just as he tipped over a garbage pail and sent it rolling under one of the tables.

Both Penny and Travis jumped a foot when Maude's voice boomed out, "What's that damn dog doing in my kitchen?"

The large woman stood in front of them, hands on her hips as she glared down at them.

"He's...he's...hungry," Travis stammered, hoping any answer was better than none.

"And I suppose you two are snooping around my kitchen, looking for cookies to steal."

Both Travis and Penny shook their heads. "We were just looking for Hobo." They could hear the dog chomping on something in the scattered garbage that sounded like a bone.

"What's that you got in your hand?" Maude asked Travis suspiciously.

"Just an airplane."

"An airplane?"

"It flies," he said, glad to get the cook's attention away from any talk about the tray of eclairs he'd ruined. "See, you put on the rubber band. Pull back. And let go."

He demonstrated and the airplane went up in the air, straight at Maude, and caught in her gray hair. She jerked at it, trying to remove it, and in that instant an unbelievable thing happened.

The wig she was wearing was pulled off and so were her glasses.

Penny let out a hysterical scream as thick dark hair spilled over Maude's face.

Maude Beaker was a man!

Swearing, he lunged at Penny, trying to clamp his large hands over her mouth, but the little girl dropped to her knees and slithered under one of the low serving tables out of his reach.

"You leave her alone!" Travis screamed. Dodging thick hands reaching for him, he cried, "Help, help!" Then he slipped and fell on some of the garbage that Hobo had spilled.

Just as Beaker reached for him, the kitchen doors

swung open. Hearing Travis's cries, Steve and Deanna ran in with alarm written on their faces.

Steve stared at the dark-haired man in Maude's overalls and apron as if he were viewing a still frame in a movie. He knew what he was seeing but he couldn't believe it.

Deanna froze for a moment and then screamed, "Penny!"

"Stay back, Deanna." Beaker waved the gun he'd drawn from the voluminous pocket of his overalls. "Game's over. I've had a bellyful of the lot of you. It's time that—"

He never finished. Steve hit him with a football tackle that sent both men crashing to the floor, and the gun spinning out of Beaker's hand.

Deanna ran to Penny and Travis huddled under a serving table. As the men fought, they crashed into a small cutting table, spilling a rack of cutlery on the floor. They lost their balance, and as they wrestled on the floor, Beaker grabbed one of the knives.

"Look out, Dad," Travis cried. "He's got a knife!"

Steve tried to roll away from the thick arm slicing the air with the knife. He wasn't quick enough. Beaker plunged the sharp blade into Steve's forearm. Blood gushed out from the open wound, and before Steve could regain his balance, Beaker landed a dizzying blow on his chin.

As Beaker jerked to his feet, he frantically looked around for his gun.

"Don't move." Deanna's finger was firmly poised on the trigger of his gun, and her voice was as cold as Arctic ice as she pointed the weapon at his head.

"Easy, easy, pretty lady," Beaker cautioned in a coaxing voice.

At that moment, Deanna was filled with such consuming rage that she didn't even hear him. *This was the man who had murdered her husband and put her daughter through months of hell.* ''You deserve to die,'' she said in a cold, unemotional voice.

''Deanna, no. Don't do it.'' Staggering to his feet, and holding his bleeding arm, Steve rushed over to her. His voice seemed to shake her out of her spell. She let him take the pistol with his one good hand, and he leveled it at Beaker.

''How about it, *Maude?* Do you want to be shot or poisoned? Or maybe you'd rather have your skull cracked the way you hit Susan?''

''It's your fault for interfering!'' Beaker lashed out. ''If you'd let the kid alone, I wouldn't have had to shut the brat up before she really put the finger on me. Hell, I wasn't even sure that she'd seen me that night until I heard she was going to a shrink so she could remember who'd been with her father that night.''

''Why did you do it, Beaker?''

''Shoot Ben? He was threatening to take my house, car and the clothes on my back to pay off a gambling loan.''

''I ought to shoot you just for putting Susan in the hospital with a skull fracture,'' Steve threatened. The telephone call for Deanna had been from the Whitcombs. Susan had regained consciousness, and had told her story to the sheriff. After stomping out of Corky's Café, she'd met Maude in the parking lot, and asked to bum a ride back to the hotel. When she got in the pickup, she picked up a box that was sitting in the front seat, and accidentally spilled the contents when she was putting it on the floor. It was filled with men's clothes, a razor and a gray wig. That's when he hit her. Even if

Susan hadn't regained consciousness, Janson's investigation had finally turned up a very interesting fact.

Roy Beaker didn't have an aunt.

Deanna grabbed a tea towel and tied it around Steve's bleeding arm as best she could. Penny and Travis were still under the table with Hobo, and Deanna had ordered them to stay there.

"The sheriff's already on his way, but I'm not sure I can keep from blowing this creep's head off." Steve's smile was coldly threatening. "Self-defense, you know."

Now it was Deanna's turn to be concerned. She truly didn't know whether or not Steve would orchestrate a move on Beaker's part so he could repay Beaker for all the heartache he had caused.

She didn't have time to decide what she should do or say, because just then Sheriff Janson and two deputies came into the kitchen. The sheriff obviously had not expected to see the scene that met him. He had intended to get to the hotel before the fireworks began. "Well, well, what do we have here—Maude?"

Beaker spit out an ugly name at him. "Give me back my gun and I'll show you."

"I'm betting this little baby will match the bullets found in Ben's body," the sheriff said as he took the gun from Steve's hand. "Roy Beaker, I'm charging you with first-degree murder and three counts of felonious assault." He nodded to his deputies. "Take him, and read him his rights."

Janson glared at Steve's bloody arm. "Is that a bullet wound?"

"No, he stabbed me with a butcher knife."

"You just couldn't leave things alone until I got here,

could you? You had to be the smart guy and unmask him yourself.''

''I didn't unmask him.''

''Then who did?''

Steve laughed and pointed to two pairs of wide rounded eyes staring at them from under the table.

''They did.''

Chapter Seventeen

Steve made the trip over Rampart Pass twice in the same day. The stab wound would need stitches, and the small first-aid station in Eagle Ridge insisted that he get treatment at the Silver Springs hospital.

"No, you stay here with the kids, Dee," Steve said firmly when she told him anxiously that she'd take him there herself. "There's no need for all of us to make that trip again. One of the sheriff's deputies is going to drive me. I'll spend the night, and someone can bring me back in the morning." Both of them were still in a state of shock over what had happened. He hated to leave her. "You're going to be all right, aren't you?"

She nodded, but she was still reeling from the adrenaline that had shot through her body. At the moment, she felt as if someone had been physically beating on her. They had brought the children back to her apartment as soon as they could, but there was little time to get their bearings because of Steve's bleeding arm.

"Travis, you're going to stay here with Penny and Dee tonight," he said gently, wondering how his son was going to handle all of this. "Will that be all right?"

"Can we still go for a chocolate malt?"

The childish innocence of the question made Steve

laugh. What a relief! The evening's high drama hadn't
fazed his son in the least. The boy had taken it in stride,
and with the resiliency of a seven-year-old, his attention
had moved onto more important things.

"I'm afraid the chocolate malts will have to wait."

"Bummer," Travis muttered.

Steve hugged him. "I promise that I'll take you and
Penny to Corky's Café just as soon as I get back."

"Okay." Travis brightened. "Hear that, Penny?" He
went over and plopped down on the sofa where she sat
clutching her toy monkey. "That means old Maude
won't be yelling at us anymore. We fixed her—him—
good, didn't we?"

The little girl searched Travis's face anxiously. "Bad
man gone?"

"Sure he's gone. Didn't you see those handcuffs? I
heard the sheriff say that he was going to lock him up
and throw away the key." Travis actually stuck out his
little chest. "I guess me and my airplane might get a
medal. What do you think, Penny? Maybe they'll give
you one, too. A big gold medal with a red ribbon. How
would you like that?"

A faint smile lifted the corners of Penny's mouth, and
Steve and Deanna let out their collective breaths. They
had been fearful that the harrowing experience might
have sent Penny back into her protective silence. With
his good arm, Steve pulled Deanna close and whispered,
"She's going to be fine."

"Yes, yes, she is," Deanna said with a spurt of hap-
piness that dispelled a familiar bone-deep chill of apprehension.

Steve wanted to stay with her, talk to her, and show
her that he was there for her, but his bleeding arm gave

him no choice. "Guess I'd better go and see to this arm before I drip blood all over your carpet."

He kissed her lightly, and there was nothing she could do but let him go. The warmth she'd felt in his arms went with him. Nothing had been said about the romantic intimacy that had flared between them, but one thing was clear. There was no reason now for him to extend his stay at the hotel.

ON THE DRIVE over the mountain pass to Silver Springs, Deputy Warring talked most of the way. A man in his fifties, he'd lived in the area most of his life, working on some of the ranches before Janson swore him in as a deputy. "I knew the Beaker family."

"And Roy?"

"Yep. He inherited a nice spread and big ranch house from his folks, but he never did work it. Sold most of the land, but kept the house. He traveled around a lot, and rumor had it that he was a cook on some merchant ship. I guess he showed up here about six months ago, but nobody connected him with Ben's murder. Of course, nobody knew about the gambling going on at the hotel either. And then, about the same time his aunt arrived, Roy took off again—at least, that's what everybody thought." The deputy shook his head. "Can you believe that guy? Who'd have thought he'd dress up like a woman, and work as a cook at the hotel?"

Nobody, thought Steve. *And he almost got away with it.*

IN SILVER SPRINGS, the deputy went with him into the hospital, waited until a doctor had dressed Steve's wound and then drove him to the Conifer Inn, where Deanna had called ahead to secure a room for him. As it turned out, it was the same room they'd had the night before.

"Back again, Dr. Sherman? Didn't you check out a few hours ago?" the desk clerk asked with undisguised curiosity as he saw the deputy's car pull away from the entrance. "Is anything the matter?"

"As a matter of fact, everything is great." He was glad that his bandaged arm was covered by his sports jacket. "I think I'll have a drink in the lounge before I go upstairs."

Since the dance floor was crowded at this late hour, and most of the tables were taken, Steve sat at the bar for a quick nightcap. As he drank a scotch and soda, his analytical mind organized the happenings of the last month, and he allowed himself a sense of professional accomplishment. In the midst of all the turmoil, he'd been able to keep Penny's therapy on track, and he was sure that with just a few follow-up sessions, the little girl would be back to her old outgoing self. He'd made some mistakes, but he'd achieved what Deanna had hired him to do.

Deanna.

He swirled the amber liquid in his glass. With the arrest of her husband's killer, she would be out from under the dark cloud that had descended upon her and her daughter. From the moment he'd met Deanna, her inner strength and resiliency had impressed him. He'd admired the way she had conducted herself in the face of false accusations and adversity, but all of that was in the past now. Nothing stood in the way of her enjoying the well-earned success of owning and managing her own hotel. She would be free to pick up her life again without any complications.

Complications.

Steve sighed. The memory of holding Deanna close and kissing her stabbed him with a poignant sense of loss. He couldn't rationalize his feelings. One thing was clear, considering everything, he should have known better than to give in to the physical attraction between them. He knew at the time that she needed him for reassurance, support and understanding. She'd never invited him to be her lover, and he should have been able to defuse the sexual chemistry that flared between them. The truth was that he wanted to take her to bed—he wanted *her*, period—but he'd better get himself back to Denver before he started something that would complicate both of their lives.

Feeling at odds with himself, Steve went upstairs to the familiar sitting room and bedroom they'd checked out of earlier in the day. The maid had put the sofa bed away, left clean towels and cleaned up all the evidence of their stay the night before, but the sight of a clean terry-cloth robe like the one Deanna had worn added to the loneliness of the room.

Steve sat on the edge of one of the beds. In his mind's eye he could see two rumpled children with their tousled heads upon a pillow, and a sexy fair-haired woman teasing his senses with her every movement.

Restless and filled with a growing discontent with himself and the whole world, he left the bedroom and strode into the sitting area. An expected reaction, he told himself. After all that had happened, anyone would be ready to climb the walls.

He jumped when the telephone rang.

When he heard Deanna's voice, his chest tightened. "Is everything all right?"

"Fine. I just wanted to make sure everything went well at the hospital."

"They stitched me up in good fashion, gave me a few pain pills and sent me on my way."

"I hope you weren't already asleep."

"Not at all. I'm having a little trouble settling down. How are the kids?"

"Sound asleep, finally. We had a lot of company after you left. I think everyone who works at the hotel came by the apartment to express their disbelief. I even got an apology from Dillon."

"Good. Things ought to be a lot easier for you now that he's willing to eat humble pie."

"I hope so." She paused. "Jeffery volunteered to watch Travis and Penny, so I'll be able to drive over and pick you up midmorning."

"Sounds good."

"Well, good night, then."

"Deanna?"

"Yes?"

"I wish you could come tonight." He was surprised that he'd spoken the thought aloud.

"So do I," she said softly and hung up.

He stared at the phone for a long time with only one thought foremost in his mind.

What a damn fool I am.

Then he started making plans.

THE NEXT MORNING, Deanna almost sent Roger to Silver Springs instead of going herself. For most of the night, she'd lain awake, thinking about Steve and weighing the temptation to have an affair with him. Even if the future only promised a long-distance relationship, they could be with each other when she took Penny into Denver for her sessions, and, undoubtedly,

Steve and Travis would make some return visits to the hotel.

Would that be enough? She had to respect his honesty about his reluctance to marry again. Eventually, the odds were strong that he'd find someone in his own social circle that would replace the wife he'd lost. But until then—?

By eleven o'clock the next morning, when she arrived at the Conifer Inn and made her way up to room 207, her decision had been made.

He answered her knock almost at once. "Hi."

"Hi," she responded, a little self-conscious.

His welcoming smile was broad, and his eyes shone with excited expectation as he stepped back, opening the door wide so that she could see into the small living room,

At first she thought she was hallucinating. Blinking several times, she wasn't sure if her eyes were in focus. Bouquets of flowers filled the room, dozens of roses and blossoms of every size and color were everywhere. The place looked like an inside garden and the air was redolent with sweet perfume.

"What on earth?" she breathed.

He gave a soft laugh. "It occurred to me last night after we hung up that I'd been lying to myself long enough." He drew her over to the sofa and sat down beside her.

She looked at him in complete bewilderment. "I don't understand."

"It's simple. I decided the place needed to be spruced up for the occasion."

"What occasion?"

He took her hand. "I'm going to propose to you."

She swallowed a sudden lump in her throat, and couldn't find the words to say anything.

He touched her cheek with caressing tenderness. "I want to marry you, Dee. I'm hopelessly and totally in love with you." His voice was husky. "Could you? Would you be my wife?"

"Now?" She looked around, half expecting a minister to appear from behind one of the tall floral arrangements.

He chuckled. "No, the flowers are for my proposal. I thought we might wait a day or two for the wedding ceremony, but not much longer," he warned. "I know this is sudden, but—"

"Yes."

The persuasive words he had prepared died in his throat.

"Yes, I'll marry you."

He searched her face and saw nothing but love shining in her eyes. "I promise you that you'll never be sorry."

Joyful tears started trailing down her cheeks, and she couldn't speak. He wanted to marry her. She didn't have to settle for less.

"I know this means giving up the Drake Hotel and moving to Denver," he said gently. "If you want another hotel to manage, we'll get it for you."

"That won't be necessary," she said, and her brimming eyes twinkled as she added, "I'll be too busy with our three children to do much else."

"Three?"

Leaning into him, she deliberately crossed a provocative leg over his. The sexual hunger that had been between them from the beginning exploded full-blown.

Her voice was husky as she said, "I believe in planning ahead."

He kissed her seductive, willing lips and murmured, "Me too." Then he picked her up in his arms and carried her into the bedroom.

Shh!

has a secret...

It's *confidential!*

September 2000

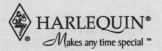

HARLEQUIN
Duets™

Romance is just one click away!

online book **serials**

➤ *Exclusive* to our web site, get caught up in both the daily and weekly online installments of new romance stories.

➤ Try the Writing Round Robin. Contribute a chapter to a story created by our members. Plus, winners will get prizes.

romantic **travel**

➤ Want to know where the best place to kiss in New York City is, or which restaurant in Los Angeles is the most romantic? Check out our Romantic Hot Spots for the scoop.

➤ Share your travel tips and stories with us on the romantic travel message boards.

romantic reading **library**

➤ Relax as you read our collection of Romantic Poetry.

➤ Take a peek at the Top 10 Most Romantic Lines!

Visit us online at

www.eHarlequin.com
on Women.com Networks

COMING NEXT MONTH

#577 A MOTHER'S SECRETS by Joanna Wayne
Randolph Family Ties

Kathi Sable was in danger. The threat of harm to loved ones had caused her to flee…not realizing she carried Ryder Randolph's child. Now, almost two years later, the forces that sent her on the run drew Kathi back to Ryder's side. Determined to reveal the truth, she needed Ryder's help to end the threat—and make their family reunion last a lifetime.

#578 RENEGADE HEART by Gayle Wilson
More Men of Mystery

Ex-government agent Drew Evans was being hunted for a crime he hadn't committed. The man who could clear Drew's name was dead, leaving his wife and daughter to take up Drew's cause. Though Drew didn't want to involve Maggie Cannon or her daughter, his life depended on questions only she could answer. But once involved, would Drew be able to let Maggie walk away? And would she want to?

#579 INADMISSABLE PASSION by Ann Voss Peterson

Five years ago, secrets shattered Brittany Gerritsen's engagement to Jackson Alcott. Now, opposing attorneys on a high-profile murder case, their exchanges heated up the courtroom—and ultimately blazed in the bedroom. Though a murderer threatened their lives, this time love just might be enough to keep them together.

#580 LITTLE BOY LOST by Adrianne Lee
Secret Identity

When someone stole her identity and her son, Carleen Ellison immediately turned to Kane Kincaid. Though she'd never told him, the child they were searching for was his and the love they'd once shared still burned in her soul. To save his boy and reclaim Carleen's love, Kane would do anything…even if it meant risking his life.

Visit us at www.eHarlequin.com

CNM07